STEP ON A CRACK, BREAK YOUR MOTHER'S BACK

Linda Kuchl Gallagher

Copyright © 2023 Linda Gallagher

All rights reserved

This is a work of fiction. Names, characters, businesses, events and incidents are the products of the author's imagination. Any resemblance to actual persons, living or dead, or actual events is purely coincidental and not intended by the author.

No part of this book may be reproduced, or stored in a retrieval system, or transmitted in any form or by any means, electronic, mechanical, photocopying, recording, or otherwise, without express written permission of the author.

To Ryan, My Wonderful Grandson and the Joy of My Life

Slowly skipping down the narrow hall and squeezing Papa's hand, her frightened eyes flicker across the row of empty straw-filled cages at Lincoln Park Zoo. Growing closer to the last cage, her ten-year-old heart pounds with anticipation and fear, knowing who is caged there. His monstrous roar resonates and echoes across the zoo when he grows angry and mightily stretches his muscular 6'2" body upright while fiercely and powerfully beating his massive long-haired chest. Bushman, the most famous, terrifying gorilla in the world.

Prying open her tightly closed eyes, she sees him docilely seated on a wooden stump, staring out at her from behind piercing black eyes in an oversized head. With an unexpected thunderous roar, he leaps through the air, throwing himself against the steel bars of his cage. Terrified and swinging around to grab Papa, she turns her head to the side only to see the beautiful, young bride patiently standing in the long line of spectators waiting her turn to view the exhibit.

Jolted awake from the terrifying nightmare, her eyes lock on the rotating blades of the old, hypnotizing ceiling fan. Long-forgotten superstitions flood back, recognizing that seeing a bride in one's dream signifies death, and she begins praying for the three women.

SISTER ELEANOR

Retrieving the outgoing mail and pushing the red flag down on the mailbox, the overworked postal worker recalls his catechism lessons as a young boy, remembering St. Philomena was the patron saint for infants and babies. With the rain pouring down and not wishing to soak the contents, he struggles to stuff the large brown envelope into the already cramped mailbox addressed to Sister Eleanor at St. Philomena's Maternity Home. When catholic charities closed their unwed mother facilities in the early 1970s, non-profit ministries like these were born and still exist today, meeting the needs of apprehensive pregnant teens.

Located on ten wooded acres in rural McHenry, Illinois, the teen girls live together in a family setting during their pregnancies. At the same time, they are taught the skills needed to build a better life for themselves and their babies in a loving and supportive community. They are taught life skills, provided counseling and given spiritual guidance to transition back into society once their baby is born.

St. Phil's is non-judgmental and provides the girl with a safe loving home, regardless if she decides to keep her baby or put the child up for adoption, while guiding her towards independence.

Founded in 1990 by a generous donation from an anonymous benefactor, four small cottages were built that each housed three to four pregnant girls. However, with fewer girls attending every year, only one house is still utilized.

Marlena, the timid postulant, plopped the damp letters and brochures on the desk of sprightly eighty-two year old Sister Eleanor Swiderski, the devoted director since the benevolent home's inception and who still manages it today.

After lowering the glasses propped on top of her snowy white hair, Sister Eleanor's knotted, arthritic hands sift through the mail. Seeing the large brown envelope, a chill runs through her old body, and she quickly places it in the bottom desk drawer and locks it away. With countless keys on the keyring clinking together, she rises from her chair and leaves the room to join Marlena for morning prayers.

Later that evening, after retrieving the envelope and alone in her solitary bedroom, she catches her breath while nervously ripping it open. Characterized by her detailed and precise nature, before removing the contents of the envelope, she reads the two pieces of correspondence she has received previously.

The first was received two weeks ago and read:

My dear Sister Eleanor,

I plead for your kindness and assistance. After much searching, I am confident my mother was a resident of St. Philomena's Maternity Home, and I was born there sometime in the fall of 1992.

Now, being thirty years old, I am engaged to be married to a wonderful man, and the need to contact my birth mother is most critical. My fiancée has a family history of cystic fibrosis, and I urgently need to speak with her about our family medical history before starting a family. Please be assured I was raised in a loving home and only wish to communicate with her regarding this vital health concern. Time is of the essence.

With love and deep gratitude, September Williams

The second letter was received one week ago and read:

Dear Sister Eleanor,

Thank you for your prompt reply. However, it shattered my faith and disappointed me that you advised that due to federal, state and church regulations, you cannot assist me in locating my birth mother. Recognizing St. Philomena's is struggling financially, I am enclosing a very generous check in the hopes you will reconsider these doctrines, which are not only archaic but cruel. Please call me at the phone number provided or contact me at the PO Box below ASAP.

September Williams

After reading the shocking letter received today, her head throbs, contemplating the difficult decision she knows is inevitable and only she can make.

Sister,

After ignorantly returning my check uncashed, I recognize the callous, sinful old woman you really are. I believe you have in your possession the information I have requested and are spitefully withholding it from me.

Having obtained a professional private investigator to further explore my circumstances, he has discerned that my birth mother was one of the first three girls to have been accepted in your facility in 1992, and all three of these girls gave birth to daughters born in September that year. One of them was me!

I have enclosed three letters sealed in envelopes, one for each of them, and a copy for you to read. I know you have pertinent information regarding these women or the means to unearth it. For your own good, I suggest you address the letters and forward them to these women to avoid having your very holy hands covered in their blood. Their lives depend on it, and so does yours, you miserable old bitch!

September

Sister Eleanor places the three lavish envelopes, sealed with gold foil embossed stickers, on her desk as she tightly grasps the arm of the chair after reading her copy.

Mother,

Growing up, my friends would laugh and wildly jump back and forth and side to side, trying to avoid stepping on the lines in the sidewalks because they didn't dare "Step on a crack and break their mother's back."

However, Mother, it was different for me. I would stretch out my tiny leg or stop short intentionally, ensuring I stepped on every crack. I would furiously jump up and down, stomping my foot on it, imagining your bones cracking and splintering, and I prayed you would feel the excruciating pain of your back breaking into thousands of pieces.

Now, having the time and means, I look forward to our reunion, when I hear you scream out in agony as I step on that final crack, shattering your back and destroying you forever.

Your daughter, September

Sister Eleanor sits down in her over-stuffed armchair, and holding the rosary beads her mother gave her so many years ago, shuts her eyes and begins to pray.

1992

Bill Clinton won the presidential election and became the 42nd President of the United States; John Gotti, the impeccably dressed head of the Gambino crime family, was sentenced to life behind bars; Michael and Scotty were piling on points as the beloved Chicago Bulls won the NBA championship for the second year in a row; and the Alphabet Girls arrived at St. Philomena's Maternity Home.

They called themselves the Alphabet Girls because of the first letter in each of their names: Amy, Beth and Christine. No one had a last name at St. Phil's. They all arrived on that same sweltering July day, which was the only thing they had in common.

AMY

Tucked in the corner of her suitcase was the crushed hand-made corsage decorated with sugar cubes that she received from her best friend Jennifer for her sixteenth birthday last month. At that time, rowdy friends and classmates greeted her in school, hugging her with choruses of "Sweet Sixteen and Never Been Kissed". The other Taft High School cheerleaders had decorated her locker with blue balloons and silver ribbons to help her celebrate, while Amy wondered if her mother back at home was trying to squeeze into her tiny cheerleading uniform.

Amy's mother didn't want to be her mother. Although twenty-two years older than Amy, she wanted to be her older sister, which was how she described herself to all the repulsive men who came in and out of their lives. Her mother was always an attractive woman and an attention seeker, but after her parents divorced, she morphed into a cheap, burnt-out Barbie doll.

After living with years of screaming, swearing and objects pitched against the walls, she wasn't saddened or upset when her parents announced they were divorcing. Her mother, showcasing her signature large dangling earrings, and her kind dad, peering over his half-glasses, sat her down, explained the circumstances, and sought to soften the blow by gifting her with a wide black leather belt from the Limited.

Both interrupting each other's conversation, they explained

that her life wouldn't change as her dad would move into a furnished apartment in their Edison Park neighborhood, and she and her mom would remain living in their comfortable Chicago-style bungalow. Things were going okay until her mom discovered that the apartment he was moving into also included her mom's best friend, Stephanie.

The first objective of her mom was to visit the hairstylist whose magic fingers transformed her warm chestnut brown hair into Vixen Platinum Blonde. Although she always had a good figure, she lost an additional ten pounds when she became a member of Bally's Fitness World. Her newly bleached teeth almost matched her hair color, and she couldn't touch Amy's face without scratching it with her long false fingernails. Investing in skinny halter tops and two sizes too small jeans, her clothes screamed, "Look at me!"

She fell in love with every man she met at the neighborhood bar and would have them move in before the week was over. The house was saturated with the smell of sex, sweat, booze and smoke, and the once-friendly neighbors now complained of the noise and the overflowing garbage cans littering the alley.

Amy was never introduced as her daughter but as her baby sister, and as she struggled just to find a quiet corner to hide and do her homework, the unshaven, sloppy perverts always seemed to find her. To them, she was not her daughter, so no boundaries needed to be set. She was just the hot younger sister whom they lusted after.

Confessing to her dad how frightened she was, he told her mother he didn't want his daughter living in such an inappropriate environment. He suggested Amy move in with him, adding that he and Stephanie had recently split up, and she could have her room. Her mother, thrilled to get rid of the competition, happily and enthusiastically agreed.

Amy's new bedroom was smaller than the one she had in the old bungalow, but there was a desk, a full-length mirror and plenty of room for her clothes and cheer outfit. It was clean, had a stocked refrigerator, Direct TV and was only a short four-block walk to school.

After what she had been experiencing living with her crazy mother, she found herself happy again and thought her life was getting back to normal. Normal for about a month, that is, until she woke up one night to the familiar smell of liquor and her father's hands traveling all over her body.

Her mom had gone from forty-six years old to sixteen years old, her dad had gone from being a ComEd lineman in Chicago to being a Clearview Energy lineman in Dallas, and Amy had gone from being the good girl who cheered for the Taft High School Eagles, who really was sweet sixteen and had never been kissed, to sitting in an unfamiliar cottage on a hard, plain bed with a baby growing inside her.

BETH

Beth called herself the almost girl. She almost lost ten pounds, she almost got a college degree, she almost got a great job and she almost got away from those brutal rapists that frigid winter night.

With the first formal week of school ending, she was pleased with herself. The poster of U2 and Bono was tacked up over her bed, the heavy books needed for her studies were neatly stacked on the tiny dorm room desk, pledging Delta Gamma was about to begin, and yet one essential item was still required – a fake ID.

Handing her the counterfeit State of Illinois driver's license, Jimmy, whose dad was a Berwyn cop, assured her it would pass even the most prudent police officer's scrutiny. Paying him, she dug out forty dollars of the cash she had earned while waiting tables at Tata's Pizza during the summer. She now felt secure and confident she could gain entry into any of the packed student bars around Illinois State University.

Having completed her first semester at ISU, she loaded the bags of dirty laundry into her dad's Jeep Cherokee, anxious to return home for Christmas break. Turning down her familiar street and seeing the sparkling Christmas tree of her childhood shining through the large picture window, holiday memories overwhelmed her. She flew up the steps, joyfully reuniting with her mother, who engulfed her in her chubby arms as she inhaled the aroma of burnt peanut butter cookies.

Fidgeting and squirming, she couldn't sit still waiting for

her dad to join them to proudly announce she made the Dean's List, then watching and grinning as their bright smiles eclipsed that of the dazzling star topping the tree.

Not fifteen minutes later, she was chatting on the phone with high school friends from Mother McCauley, catching up on their college experiences and the latest neighborhood gossip. They all felt so much more adult and exhibiting newfound independence since returning from college, they eagerly organized a girls night out to celebrate the holidays at the Artful Dodger, one of the da bomb hot spots in the Chicago inner city.

The following day, loaded down with shopping bags and gifts, after spending the busy morning Christmas shopping on State Street with her mom and sister, they stood patiently in line at Marshall Field's, waiting to be seated in the elegant Walnut Room. While viewing the gloriously decorated 45-foot Great Tree and listening to familiar piped-in Christmas music, each one excitedly anticipated that first bite of legendary, mouth-watering chicken pot pie.

Afterward, with snow-flakes starting to swirl from the sky, her mom was anxious to return home before her dad, a Chicago cop who worked narcotics in the lethal and deadly Gresham District, left for work because she superstitiously believed her kiss on his cheek would keep him safe. Too bad she didn't reserve that kiss for Beth.

Shortly after her dad headed for work, she called Erin to see if everyone was still on for tonight, even with the weather report calling for five inches of snow. Considering the uncertain forecast and after speaking with the other enthusiastic girls, it was unanimous that northside dudes were about to discover that southside girls could party with the best of them.

Carefully pulling up the ankle zippers on the bottom of her tight Guess jeans, she smiled after winning the argument with her wary mother. Her mom promised not to tell her dad she was going into the city, but the deal breaker was she could not drive her car.

Impatiently waiting to be picked up and gazing into the

night sky, she notices the snowflakes are growing fatter and falling faster, and it is 9:30 PM by the time long-time friends Erin, Ann and Toni finally drive up, stuffed into Erin's little green Ford Pinto.

Leaping into the auto, there are hugs and screams of excitement from the friends after not seeing each other for months. Before pulling out, Ann questions if Beth has her fake ID warning that the popular dark and murky bar has buzzkill bouncers notorious for "talking to the hand". In other words, they were intolerant, refusing to hear any excuses, and if your ID didn't pass their inspection, you were under no circumstances gaining entry into the bar.

The Artful Dodger and Bucktown were light years away from the bastion of their tight-knit community, especially if you were a car full of naive teenage girls on a snowy winter night.

Although the gentrification of Bucktown started slowly in the 1980s, in 1992, many sections were still considered unsafe and dangerous areas of Chicago with frequent violent crimes and growing numbers of explosive street gangs claiming their turf, notably the savage Latin Kings.

After parking the auto, each taking a turn checking their hair and makeup in the visor mirror, the girls giggled and fought their way through the blowing snow for three dark blocks to the entrance of the celebrated bar.

Intoxicated by the excitement of the booming, pulsating music heard on the street and the hot boys mulling around the entrance, eyeing them, they found themselves getting pushed and separated in the huge crowd trying to gain entry into the club. Toni, the tallest, waved her arms and attempting to shout over the noise, yelled for everyone once in the club to meet at the dance floor in the rear of the bar.

Beth's friends smiled and flirted with the burly bouncer checking IDs and joyously danced their way inside to the beat of rap music. However, when she timidly produced her fake ID, the bouncer's eyes turned sharp while scrutinizing her, and flinging the license back at her, acidly blurted out, "Vamoose sweetheart," and tossed her out of line.

Horrified and unable to see her friends, she is rudely pushed back onto the street. Afraid and not knowing what to do, and with no phone booth in sight to call home, she decides to walk back down Wabansia Avenue to try and locate the car.

Alone late at night, with her feet freezing and red hair flying wildly, she grows more frightened, feeling trapped in this unfamiliar neighborhood. The horrible realization hits her that she is worlds away from her safe haven neighborhood of Mt. Greenwood, home of the South Side Irish and countless police officers and firefighters, who were always on guard and protected each other.

Becoming more alarmed while eyeing the deteriorating homes, abandoned buildings and vandalized cars lining the garbage-strewn street, she searches for Erin's car, not knowing what she will do if she finds it.

With the snow starting to subside and the wind quieting down, she is horror-stricken, hearing deep male voices taunting her as they follow close behind. Slipping, as she tries to hurry, she hears the snow crunching as heavy footsteps come chasing after her.

A powerful push from behind sends her crashing to the ground, and painfully lifting her head to the right; she gapes at an expensive gray and red Nike forcefully trapping her to the ground. At the same time, a singular blue Nike kicks her hard in the face as the chilling words echo in her throbbing ear, "Girl, whatcha doin' all alone?"

Yanking her hair and dragging her to her feet, they laugh like hyenas while attempting to squeeze her breasts through her thick goose-down jacket. Both skinny Latino men wear gold and black unzipped jackets and have Latin King crown tattoos on their dirty necks and tear-drop tattoos under their drugged-out eyes, which Beth knows from her father means they have killed or spent hard time in prison.

Longing to be home with her family, she sobs and pleads with them to let her go while slipping in the slushy snow, trying to escape, but it is no match when they callously drag her into the dingy gangway.

Trying to fight one of them off, he angrily slips the sharp knife under her soft skin, yanking it up and ripping open the side of her neck, while the other throws his head back, laughing hysterically. All hope deserting her; they take turns slicing off her clothes while all she can do is focus on their untied, expensive athletic shoes, praying she survives.

Taking turns forcefully thrusting into her while the other's disgusting hands muffle her screams from the unbearable pain, they mercifully stop and light up their joints after they both have finished assaulting her and zip up.

Lying face down, exposed in the snow, she prays the ordeal is over, only to be harshly flipped over. Having her bruised breast grabbed once again, she stares in absolute horror as she watches the jagged knife, as if in slow motion, swoop down, taking aim at her breast and expertly slicing off her nipple, while the two of them roar in amusement at the bloody souvenir.

She is thankful for the freezing snow rapidly burying her as it numbs the pain and clots the blood flowing from her ravaged body. Wincing in agony and shamefully humiliated, she staggers out from the disgusting alley where she has been dragged and left to die.

Half-naked and bleeding, she gropes her wrist for the costly Swatch, a graduation gift from her beloved grandmother, but it is no longer there. Nor is the black fringed bucket bag she begged her sister to loan her for this special night, and she prays the distant echo of a police car siren is her worried father speeding to rescue her.

Since that unspeakable night, men, women and even children's athletic shoes have become a disturbing obsession with her, and carrying her one piece of Samsonite luggage into the already occupied room of the small cottage, she notes not the sad pregnant girl sitting on the bed, but her swollen feet squeezed into the brand-new pair of white, red-stitched Keds sneakers.

CHRISTINE

Jolting the elderly parishioner, whose eyes were fluttering shut, Reverend Calvin Livingston pounds the lectern, causing Mr. Howell's eyes to immediately fly open. The wall clock at the rear of the church shows it is nearing noon, and needing to leave immediately, he concludes services by admonishing his parishioners of the cunning devil, continuously trying to enter their hearts and minds while repeating how much Jesus loves them.

Tossing his vestment over the chair, he has no doubts he will locate a parking spot on Irving Park Road and be seated in Schulien's Restaurant well before the arrival of his blind date set up by his friend, the choirmaster.

However, Loretta, the plain, ordinary-looking forty-seven-year-old head teller at Lake View Trust and Savings, is already seated in a cozy corner booth when he opens the door. She timidly smiles and waves to him, while both kind, considerate people hold hopeful expectations, realizing their chances for marriage and children are nearing their expiration dates.

Surprising friends, family and parishioners, not in love but settling for each other, Pastor Livingston pays the clerk ten dollars for the marriage license fee. Standing before a judge in Marriage Court at Chicago City Hall, they promise until death due them part, and with his strict sect tightly adhering to the old doctrine, Calvin hopes his new wife will comply.

Almost nine months to the date of their marriage, Christine

was born to two wonderful people who were loving parents to a baby and toddler but were too old and poorly equipped to understand and control a spirited teenage daughter.

As a child, she sat quietly next to her mother in the front pew, clutching her stuffed giraffe and appearing to be listening intently to Calvin preaching his fire and brimstone sermons. Growing older, she was expected to attend services every Wednesday and Friday evening. On Sundays, there was Sunday school, church services and always a boring dinner of dry meatloaf at some elderly parishioner's home.

Being raised in the strict sect her father observed, her parents frowned on her listening to music, dancing, wearing make-up, swearing and prohibited her from walking to the Music Box Theater with the other girls to sigh over Tom Cruise in *A Few Good Men*.

Attending 8th grade at Blaine Grammar School, her parents forbade her to attend the Friday night teen center dances held in the gymnasium. Angry and exhausted from fighting with her parents, she found it easier to lie that she was studying with Becky and then leave together to meet up with the other kids and dance wildly to the blaring electric sounds of Bon Jovi, GunsNRoses and Kid Rock. Her friends marveled that someone like Christine, who was forbidden to dance, could shake her body as sensually as any senior in high school.

Her parents constantly fought the battle to keep Christine from growing up, but she always found ways to outsmart them. Forbidden to wear make-up, which would be impossible to hide from her inflexible parents, she was only allowed to curl her long eyelashes, blanketing her stunning blue eyes.

Although her mother fought, by keeping her dressed in Disney princess clothing, lacey white anklets and Hello Kitty jewelry, it was impossible to hide her stunning beauty, boasting a flawless complexion, high cheekbones and long, luxurious blonde hair.

After breakfast each morning, her parents would join hands and pray over her. Standing on the front porch steps, their eyes would follow her as she walked down Grace Street on her way to school. Out of their sight, she was quick to roll up her pleated skirt, pull out the rhinestone earrings from her pocket and pinch her cheeks as she shimmied down the sidewalk.

Christine was very aware of her beauty, and on the walk to school, she constantly spun her head whenever hearing a car approaching from behind to catch the face of her latest admirer while anticipating how long it would take to hear the long, sharp wolf whistle or intent beep from the horn.

However, with all her worldly looks and ideas, she was very naive and still childlike. If it hadn't been for Becky or Mrs. Stamer's health class at school, she wouldn't have known about her period. She was thirteen years old, and her mother still had not mentioned it.

It was becoming riskier and more difficult to fool her irritating, saintly parents, and tonight with the Christmas Tinsel Twirl dance being held at the Lincoln Belmont YMCA for the older, cool high school kids, she and Becky planned to crash.

Propping her Aladdin sleeping bag under her arm, she jokingly told her parents not to miss her too much, giggling and lying that she would probably get no sleep while attending Becky's sleepover because they would be up late singing along with their favorite Disney videos.

However, what was really on her mind was how cool she would look tonight in the red low-cut holiday dress secretly purchased with her confirmation money from Lord & Taylor. She hoped it wasn't too wrinkled, having hidden it behind Becky's not near-as-sexy green taffeta dress in Becky's over-stuffed closet.

Tightly grasping the handrail, attempting to keep her balance in the pointy sling-back black heels, she climbed the stairs to the second floor and stared in astonishment, eyeing the huge YMCA gymnasium strung with tiny white twinkling lights, red and green crepe-paper streamers and a giant spinning mirrored disco ball. The room was packed with older kids going berserk, gyrating to George Thorogood's frenzied *Rock and Roll*

Christmas.

However, excitement quickly changed to disappointment for the excited girls. Even with painstakingly applied black eyeliner and hot pink lip gloss, they still looked like 8th graders, and they were embarrassed and humiliated after being snubbed and ignored by the older mocking teens.

Frustrated, slipping off their shoes, they sulked downstairs to the first-floor game room after hearing the echoes of a ping pong ball ricocheting across the table to find tough guys Gino Falco and Sean Flynn, the two most popular boys in their class, sweating, back-handing and bashing a banged-up ping pong ball.

Whatever the older kids upstairs didn't appreciate, the boys downstairs definitely did. Tossing their rackets on the table, they gawked at the girls in amazement while picking up their hoodies from the scuffed floor and arrogantly walked over to join them.

The dejected girls, realizing they had struck out upstairs with no invite to a romantic high school afterparty in a dark basement, settled on an invitation for a sausage and mushroom pizza from Biasatti's and watching the creepy *Silence of the Lambs* on VHS with the immature boys.

Cigarette butts, old newspapers and broken glass littered the filthy stairs to Gino's third-floor apartment, and the girls made a face at each other with the disgusting reek of cigarette smoke permeating the gross apartment.

After a few minutes, Gino slyly pulled a half-empty bottle of Jim Beam and some used paper cups from behind his back. Sensing bad vibes, Becky fiercely shook her head no and declined, but Christine, always willing to break her parent's strict rules, was all in.

Stifling how awful the gold liquid burned and tasted, Christine raised her cup for a refill while the boys laughed and egged her on. Growing exceedingly uncomfortable, Becky announced she was going home while Christine scowled at her good friend, calling her a loser and pathetic goody-two-shoes.

She begged Christine to go home with her, but after continually refusing to leave, she reluctantly left without her. At the same time, Sean decided to join Becky walking down congested Southport Avenue just as the snow started to fall.

Christine, now alone with Gino, reached for his hand, hoping it would slow down the spinning room as she tried to concentrate on the disturbing *Silence of the Lambs*. Unable to keep her eyes open, she was startled and woke up when she felt the zipper on the back of her dress being unzipped and his hand struggling to unhook her bra.

Gino confessed he had loved her since fifth grade, and realizing she had a crush on him, continued with the line countless teenage boys for decades have used that never grew old. He told her that if she loved him, this was the perfect time for her to prove it. Still dizzy from the alcohol and enjoying the new feelings she never knew existed, she let him continue.

It was the first time for him also, by the look on his anxious face, and he reassured her it was scientifically proven that a virgin couldn't get pregnant the first time she had sex. Scared yet exhilarated, Christine was enjoying how she felt as they explored each other's bodies, and since she had never had a period, she awkwardly experienced her painful, messy unsatisfying first time.

Afterward, she proudly thought about how she would boast to her girlfriends that she was probably the first of her friends to experience sex. Another first she couldn't possibly be aware of, however, was her budding body ovulating for the first time.

Her mother, noticing her blossoming breasts, uncomfortably read to her from The Christian Girl's Guide to Growing Up and embarrassingly pronounced the four-syllable word menstruation, and six months later, Dr. Chiaukulis would confirm the cancerous tumor her parents so feared was actually a growing fetus.

Christine's elderly parents never stepped out of the old Pontiac but callously dropped her off in front of St. Philomena's on the hot, humid day and immediately sped off. Her confused, bewildered eyes stayed glued to the dust kicked up from the gravel road till the car disappeared.

Sister Eleanor swung open the screen door to the stuffy cottage, seeing both Amy and Beth sitting barefoot in front of the noisy floor fan, having already introduced themselves to each other. Holding Christine's shaking hand while tears and perspiration streak down her young, innocent face, she kindly introduces her to the other girls.

Christine places a large A&P shopping bag next to the vacant bed she now climbs onto. Her blank eyes stare zombie-like, listening with the other girls to Sister Eleanor's welcome orientation as she clutches a giant, brown giraffe tightly to her tender breasts.

SEPTEMBER

Indeed, money talks! Had I only been a little more patient. I would have received the answer to my burning question before trudging to the post office and mailing the three envelopes to the ridiculous old nun.

Through the sordid and seedy Dark Web, along with a hefty amount of money, I easily found my unforgivable bitch of a mother. Small world. Knowing what I know now, I may have run into the tramp over the past thirty years while following a homerun ball launched over the Wrigley Field fence onto Waveland Avenue, swaying to the soul music of Alicia Keys on a warm summer night at Northerly Island or even lathering sun tan lotion on my arms at Riviera Beach in Lake Geneva because we lived in such close proximity of each other.

It crossed my mind to retrieve the letters also sent to the two women who were not my mother, but on second thought, I'm probably doing their daughters a favor by letting them squirm a little for their own callous decisions of thirty years ago.

The time has come, Mother, for you to feel my full fury as I step on that final crack to permanently break your back and joyfully witness your casket being lowered deep into the ground where you can rot in hell.

AMY

Slouched down and hidden behind the crude embankment, her hand clasped tightly over the youngest child's mouth, she prays the family will not be discovered. As the young soldier patrolling and scanning the rooftop approaches, she gasps when the family is suddenly caught in the ominous spotlight. He blows his shrill whistle to alarm his comrades, and the family knows they must flee immediately. Grabbing the small child's hand and leaping up, she clumsily plows into the plywood wall, causing it to crash to the floor, triggering gales of laughter and snickering, and Amy yells a loud, disgusted "Cut" from across the stage.

What was comedic during rehearsal could be catastrophic if this critical escape scene from *The Sound of Music* produced these same guffaws and laughter from the audience at the Meridian Theater in Lincolnshire. Poppy Dee, with her exquisite voice and flawless motion throughout the dance sequences, could not muster through a scene without a physical fumble.

Amy had a mediocre career as a singer and dancer in the Chicago Arts Community. Still, with a keen and observant eye, it was evident her true calling was that of a skillful stage director. She began with little theater productions of community plays at The Porchlight Music Theater in River North, and she has risen to her latest and most meaningful gig as director for the Meridian Theater production of *The Sound of Music*.

Fed up and calling for a thirty-minute break to repair the

prop, she heads to her office to brew a cup of soothing green tea. Rushing past and bumping into her, the exhausted production assistant, Donna Kemp, hands her what seems to be an elegant wedding invitation.

She is not surprised as she regularly receives wedding invites from the multitude of young performers she has worked with over the years. Sitting down at her cluttered desk, she opens the invitation, curiously wondering who of her acquaintances is marching down the aisle, and sadly realizes her boyfriend Andrew of ten years still has not popped the question.

Terrified and gasping in shock after absorbing the horrific content of the hateful letter, she flinches when Poppy suddenly appears teary-eyed, once again offering another profuse apology. Amy puts forth her best acting skills as she strives to act normal, but she is reminded of what she has fought so hard to forget all these years that she has a daughter Poppy's age.

Wanting to believe this is some sick individual's idea of a joke, but recognizing Sister Eleanor's neat script handwriting, she knows she must call and speak with her when she returns home this evening.

It is already dark when she climbs the high steps of the impressive gray stone two-flat she has labored so hard to afford and maintain. Two matching Terra Cotta planters, perched on opposite ends of the porch, bursting with flowering rose hibiscus, welcome her, while a "Neighborhood Watch – We Call the Police" sign hangs in the center of the side window.

Hearing the deadbolt snap open, she turns at the sound of a honking horn. A newer model black Camaro, with dark tinted windows, has pulled up directly in front of her building, and seeing no one else around, Amy assumes it is trying to get her attention. Not knowing anyone with this type of vehicle and being unable to see who the driver is through the blackened windows, she knows she would be crazy to approach it.

She ignores the driver, and the honking stops as she hurriedly enters her apartment. Nearly tripping on the oriental rug as she rushes to the front window, she pushes aside the old-style lace curtain to peek out to see if the unfamiliar car has gone. As if the driver has been spying on her, the unrelenting honking begins again, and she grows more frightened.

She may be frightened, but her 6'4, 260-pound bodybuilder neighbor certainly isn't, and fifteen minutes later, he and his pit bull, Felony, charge straight at the honking vehicle. At breakneck speed, the car accelerates, nearly plowing into the #152 bus as it madly cuts into the hectic traffic on Addison Street.

BETH

The roar stormed like a hurricane raging through Florida, explosive and furious. "Where is effin Ooh La La," bellowed Captain Washington striding into the bustling workplace of 25th District Police Headquarters. Other duty clerks and patrol officers hiding behind computer screens or fleeing the room clam up.

Chicago police detective Elizabeth Crowley had earned that nickname fifteen years ago. Eyeing the sensual, fiery Beth, a strung-out gang banger had stupidly grabbed her breast during a drug raid while puckering his lips and lustfully muttering, "Ooh La La" causing him to instantly be at the receiving end of a powerful, lethal swing from her nightstick, painfully splintering the bone in his knee cap. The other undercover cops, hearing this, immediately picked up on it, spreading it throughout the district, and it has remained her tag ever since.

Rivaling any Chicago St. Paddy's Day queen, blessed with copper red hair and striking green eyes, she saunters into the room in typical attire, a Metallica T-shirt clinging to her beautiful breasts and tight, ripped designer jeans, asking, "Whaz up Cap?"

Bellowing loudly but having respect for one of his senior detectives procuring the highest volume of convicted cases in the district, he spits out, "You! Torres is bitching again that you're hostile and intimidating to both her and the dog. Let it go! Now Crowley!" Walking away, he can't conceal his annoyance while leaving a trail of spilled coffee on the way back to his office.

Canine Officer Jessica Torres and her dog Magnum were thorns stuck deep in her side. Standing just over five feet tall, Torres was timid and whiney, afraid to speak up for herself but quick to run to her superiors to complain and bellyache. The photo of her spotlighting her large doe eyes and twenty-four-carat smile, which recently splashed across the top of the Chicago Tribune's "Ordinary Heroes" feature, caused her to believe she had earned the honor of CPD's personal homecoming queen.

However, the article did not include how she, a ten-year veteran of the force, had lost control of the powerful canine, who, after breaking away from her, brutally attacked a thirteen-year-old shoplifter at a Portage Park Osco. Embarrassed and humiliated, she chased after the zigzagging leash and, arriving late, finally dislodged the ferocious dog from the bloody, gnawed arm of the hysterical boy.

Twice now, the damn German Shepherd had aggressively stormed at Beth, snarling with his nose and lips curled up and white fangs exposed, while Torres seemed unable or maybe unwilling to control him.

The other officers snicker and return to their computer screens while new recruit Vicky Alvarado is going desk to desk distributing mail and hands Beth an envelope. Stunned and sickened after tearing it open and reading it, her "fuck" could have been heard across the entire 25th District. Grabbing her gray hoodie and the envelope, she storms out of the room.

Taking a shortcut through lock up, her eyes bore into Torres coyly flirting with a scruffy bail bondsman while ignoring the intimidating German shepherd sitting at attention beside her. Magnum, sensing Beth, springs up on his muscular hind legs, snarling and gnashing his teeth, blindsiding Torres, who battles to get control of him while Beth smirks and brashly saunters by. Raising her arm and pointing her harmless finger gun directly at the dog, she pulls the trigger, causing Jessica's head to nearly explode.

Not saying a word, she heads to the furthest point in the parking lot, pulls out her phone and Googles St. Philomena's in Woodstock, IL, while the freckles across her nose seem primed and ready to fight.

CHRISTINE

Joining his mother in the picturesque flower garden, eight-year-old Matthew flings an elaborate envelope to her frisbee style while she is busy plucking weeds sprouting between red and purple zinnias. Christine, mopping off the sweat dripping down her forehead and needing a break from the hot sun, pulls off her grubby garden gloves and strolls toward the swing hanging at the end of the exquisite wrap-around porch of her elegant Lake Zurich home.

Sitting beside his mother, he wonders what could possibly be in the pretty envelope. Eight-year-old athletic Matthew tops the ladder of her four sons, followed by shy, studious six-year-old Mark, rambunctious four-year-old Luke and two-year-old terror John.

Their father, Charles, an influential lobbyist for the Children Free from Harm Foundation, was no doubt just now hearing the United aircraft's wheels lowering to the ground, preparing for landing at Regan Airport in Washington, DC.

Following the incident in 1992, Christine returned home, with her absence being explained to the congregation that she was miraculously in remission after spending months in treatment for childhood leukemia at Children's Memorial Hospital on Lincoln Avenue. Her disgraced parents only referred to her pregnancy as the incident, forbidding any mention of it ever again, except for their constant reminder of the humiliation and dishonor she had brought to their family.

She was no longer the bold, flashy girl and returned home just the opposite. Prim, modest and conservative, she played down her good looks by never wearing make-up and keeping her gorgeous blonde hair chopped short.

She presumed she would be attending Lake View High School that fall. However, her parents unexpectedly enrolled her in St. Scholastica Academy, a private all-girls catholic high school, where after four years, the only accomplishment listed in her senior yearbook was that of the National Honor Society, bare of any athletics, social organizations or extra-curricular activities.

After graduating with honors, she attended Olivet Nazarene University in Bourbonnais, IL, graduating with degrees in religion and education; however, she had few outside activities and even fewer friends.

Professor Charles King, who taught biblical and theological studies at the university, was charismatic, engaging and ten years older than Christine, and it would be almost fifteen years later until their paths crossed again at the Hudson News & Gifts Shop in busy O'Hare Airport. Standing in line to purchase the current issue of People Magazine, Christine was curious to read about the deaths of Robin Williams and Joan Rivers, who died within weeks of each other. Fresh from a divorce, Professor King recognized her immediately while standing in line behind her, waiting to pay for his Wall Street Journal. After striking up a conversation, and with both their flights delayed by a colossal snowstorm now burying the runways, they sat together, talking and gazing out the huge windows at the snow drifts beginning to pile up.

He shared he was no longer married nor teaching but having retired five years earlier was now a lobbyist in Washington, DC advocating for children who were permanently abandoned and living on the streets having no safe haven and being vulnerable prey for predators.

He promised to call her when he returned from DC, and he did just that. Six months later, he walked down the aisle for the third time, and Christine was thrilled with the opportunity to leave the exhausting teaching profession and the prospect of becoming a stay-at-home wife and mother.

With it so close to lunchtime, she returns to the house to gather her, as she fondly refers to them, "Little Disciples" for lunch. While serving the BLTs, she reminds the rowdy boys that Tammy, their babysitter, will watch them this afternoon when she drives into the city to visit Granny at the Central Baptist Home.

This was a punishing duty and chore, not something she desired or enjoyed engaging in. Ten years ago, shortly after her father had a nervous breakdown and left the church, her parents, like flowers cruelly yanked from the ground, both wilted and deteriorated, with her father dying of a heart attack and her mother suffering a debilitating stroke shortly afterward.

Driving through the nightmare traffic of the Chicago expressways, she arrives at the facility around 3 PM and locates her mother sitting in the bright and cheerful recreation room with her bible on her lap. Christine approaches, offering an uncomfortable hug, while her mother recoils from her touch. Mama could never get over the incident and has never forgiven her.

Their wordless visit is only interrupted by the sound of her cell phone and an alarmed Tammy shrieking into her ear that Mark has flushed his favorite Hot Wheels car down the toilet, causing it to overflow with water spilling across the bathroom floor. Nothing new, as this is her mischievous son's modus operandi, and having the plumber on speed dial, she advises Tammy she will contact him immediately and for her to stay calm and toss some towels on the sopping floor.

While explaining the situation to the plumber, she receives another call from Dana Rae, her husband's executive assistant, which she lets go to voicemail. She later learns, after listening to Dana Rae's apologetic message, that her husband must stay an additional night in DC, and he will explain when he calls her back later this evening.

Believing she has completed her daughterly duty, after an hour of discomfort for the both of them, Christine pops two Excedrin, hoping to relieve her excruciating migraine, and woodenly says goodbye to her mother.

Waiting for the sluggish train to pass on Dee Road, she spots the all-but-forgotten envelope she had hurriedly tossed on the seat of the Audi before leaving earlier today. Drained from the visit with her mother, she sits back, slips a piece of spearmint gum into her mouth and reaches over to open it.

Shocked and sick after reading the cruel and disturbing letter, she pulls off to the side and throws up while the ear-splitting clanging from the flashing railroad crossing gates seems to cackle and scream that she will never be allowed to escape the shameful incident of her past.

THE REUNION

Beth was the first to contact Sister Eleanor, and the other two Alphabet Girls were quick to follow. With Christine being the only one unwilling to participate in a Zoom call, fearful her older children could overhear the conversation, even above the chaotic household noise, it was decided to meet at Walker Brothers Pancake House on Rand Road in Lake Zurich.

Sprightly at eighty-two years old and still driving her 2010 Honda, Sister is the first to arrive. Seated on the comfortable red window seat at the restaurant, each time the sound of the door opens, her head pops up, and she tries to guess if it is one of the girls: Amy, the talented, athletic cheerleader; Beth, the damaged college student or Christine, the timid child.

Beth is late and last to arrive, as she rushes through the door with her eyes turned down, searching and exploring the diverse mixture of shoes positioned on the hardwood floor of the restaurant. This obsession was born all those years ago when she could only survive the horrific rape by concentrating and focusing on every characteristic and detail of her attackers filthy, blood-stained obscene shoes.

She instinctively spies the black scuffed SAS orthopedic shoes, Coach Signature loafers and Jimmy Choo sandals as her worn Nikes squeak while navigating across the floor, knowing she has found the Alphabet Girls.

Eyes up now and looking forward, she spots Amy first. She is dressed in an exquisite floral chiffon maxi dress draping perfectly down her willowy, slender body and wearing white Jimmy Choo ankle strap sandals while carrying a matching bucket bag. Her ebony shoulder-length hair, with long curtain bangs, balances her heart-shaped face perfectly, and she is void of any jewelry.

Christine, a mother of four and much more practical, hides her perfect figure in Ralph Lauren beige linen ankle pants, a size too large, and an oversized matching striped Henley shirt. Wearing her medium-length chestnut brown hair in a blunt bob and just a minimal amount of make-up, as hard as she tries, she can't conceal her beauty.

Beth, caring not a whit about fashion, is wearing her favorite #79 Jose Abreu White Sox jersey and black skinny pants. Her dark copper hair cascading from a high-top ponytail swishes left and right as she joins the group. Surprisingly, she wears more make-up than the others with black mascara, making her natural dark lashes even longer and drawing attention to her emerald cat eyes while inducing lustful admirers to stare at her secretly.

Now that Sister Eleanor no longer wears her traditional black veil and dresses in conventional clothing, the middle-aged waitress placing glasses of water in front of the silent women presumes it must be a serious occasion with three worried granddaughters supporting their solemn grandmother.

The typical giddy exuberance usually expressed in a reunion after thirty years is not echoed by any of the Alphabet Girls. Instead, few adjectives and adverbs are employed when circling the table as the uncomfortable women take turns describing their current lives. None are willing to share too much information. Afterward, they sit in silence, finishing their waffles and pancakes, uncomfortably staring at each other and dabbing syrup off their lips.

Sister speaks first, addressing the immediate situation, expressing her deep concern and worries about how this nightmarish predicament could gravely impact one of their lives, not only for them individually but for their innocent families. She assures the women neither she, St. Philomena's, nor the Archdiocese would willingly provide any confidential information regarding any of them from thirty years ago.

Further affirming she has taken supplementary precautions by contacting the Chicago Joseph Cardinal Bernardin Archives and Records Center on Monroe Street in Chicago, advising they take extra precautions for any newly attempted requests being made from outside sources to gain access to the women's history. She prays this is just a cruel hoax but fears in her heart and soul that it is not.

Addressing the nightmarish mystery, none of the three girls can think of anything they have caused in their pasts to warrant such hatred. Furthermore, they all seem to have moved on and led exemplary lives.

Staring at her cold, half-eaten waffle, Christine reluctantly discloses she has never confessed to her husband she is the mother of an illegitimate child nor the circumstances leading up to 1992. She agonizes that she now fears by keeping in touch with the group, her secret could somehow escape destroying his powerful career of protecting and fighting for damaged children.

After debating if Sister Eleanor could be in some danger, upon leaving, the alliance decides to keep this information only amongst themselves. After exchanging cell phone numbers, they promise to contact each other only in case of an emergency.

AMY

Listening to the female voice on the GPS directing her back to the Meridian Lincolnshire Resort, Amy glumly realizes any chance of impressing that group with her borrowed Jimmy Choo sandals was a colossal failure. Beth would probably never want to be caught dead in them, much less be able to walk in them without hitting the ground; Sister Eleanor, slightly hard of hearing, recognizing Choo, would respond with a sincere "God bless you"; and Christine, the only one who could probably line her closet with them, judging by the 4-karat rock weighing down her left hand, would rather push her shopping cart around the dress racks at TJ Maxx.

She hopes she will have better results with the borrowed shoes tonight, impressing Andrew's parents, who will join them for dinner and attend tonight's performance of the *Sound of Music* and the award presentation afterward. Following tonight's final curtain call, Chicago stage critic Alan Stern will present Amy the coveted Midwest Guild Directors Award, recognizing outstanding artistic theatre and stage achievements in conjunction with her becoming one of Chicagoland's most sought-after theatre directors.

Being one of the rare times the two couples have shared a night out together, she crosses her fingers that Chef Franz of Willis Brew and Bistro grills the Chateaubriand to perfection, that everyone in the audience courteously turns off their cell phones during the performance and that the charming Poppy

Dee, starring in the lead role of Maria, gets through the night without a catastrophe.

She unlocks the door to her office thirty minutes before dinner reservations when Andrew and his parents, Brett and Claudine Chambers, are set to arrive. Happily kicking off the tight shoes, she grabs her makeup bag and walks barefoot to the performers dressing room, where the lighting is much brighter to freshen her makeup, and to slip into her spectacular one-shoulder, body-hugging, black-and-white shimmer gown.

Entering the room, she finds a distraught Poppy with her head down on the messy dressing table, upset and in tears. "Oh God, not now," she thinks. The last thing she needs is a blubbering, depressed Maria. Taking the time and consoling her regarding the only so-so review she received in the Chicago Tribune Arts & Entertainment Section, Amy frantically realizes she should already be at the restaurant greeting Andrew and his parents.

Sprinting back to her office to claim her shoes, she finds the door locked. With no time to spare, she desperately dials her production assistant, Donna Kemp, knowing she is never without her jangling ring of keys that can unlock any and every door of the theatre. Donna, who is not only her essential right-hand gal but also her left-hand gal, appears out of nowhere, breathing heavily, and bursts the door open, only for Amy to discover in horror the perfect designer sandals are missing from where she left them and are nowhere to be found.

Claudine's striking cropped silver hair crowns the flawless beauty of a woman her age, who is still capable of turning heads. But try as she may, she is afraid her violet eyes have betrayed her. She is stunned to see Amy gracefully walking toward their table, looking beautiful and elegant in the breathtaking shimmer dress while squeezed into a worn-out pair of black flats from Payless.

Yes, in Chef Franz's own words the dinner was "Wunderbar", the play went off without a hitch, and she crushed it with her acceptance speech, but she is still inconsolable about the missing sandals.

With the Lincolnshire Daily Herald having sent their best photographer to cover the event and grasping how fashion-conscious the women of the glitzy North Shore are, they will be clamoring tomorrow to see what designer clothing the prominent director wore at this significant social event. She can only imagine half the socialites in town throwing their heads back in laughter and ridicule when their haughty eyes spot the unflattering, gauche shoes she fought to hide under her gorgeous, sexy gown.

Being the last to exit the theatre and locking up, she now sits slumped over in Andrew's silver Lexus with her fingers clutching the cold marble base of the prestigious award sitting on her lap. Her make-up has all but vanished from the intermittent tears on the arduous thirty-mile drive home, and she remains closed off to him when he parks in front of her dark, eerie two-flat hiding behind the shadows cast from the enormous catalpa tree.

Giving it one final try, he again attempts to assure her she has no reason to be humiliated because neither Alan Stern, the audience, and least of all his mother, paid any attention to her wearing the borrowed shoes of her production assistant as all were applauding her achievement and giving her a well-deserved standing ovation when she strode across the stage to accept the award.

Accepting his tender hug and sweet kiss, she expresses she would prefer he not stay the night because her only wish is to be left alone to scarf down a couple of Extra Strength Tylenol PM and forget the day as quickly as possible. Always the gentleman, and it being so late, he suggests he walk her to her front door, but she begs him to go and curtly assures him she is quite capable of getting into her own apartment by herself. With his patience wearing thin, he shakes his head, informing her to call him tomorrow when she is hopefully in a better mood and peels down Addison Street.

Standing alone on the deserted street so late at night, she suddenly feels vulnerable and dashes up the steps, reaching the top of the porch just as a suspicious car slowly crawls by with its headlights turned off.

After hiding most of the night behind thick clouds, the moon suddenly appears, and she spots a sinister brown bag propped up against the bottom of the front door. Guided by the dim moonlight, throwing long menacing shadows across the porch, she slowly and suspiciously reaches down to pick it up and cautiously opens it. Her pounding heart races as she reaches into the mysterious paper sack, and her jarring scream pierces the night after grasping hold of the missing Jimmy Choo sandals, now cut and slashed into pieces.

****

Three days have passed since the awards ceremony. Amy looks forward to taking the next few days off from work, having toiled and labored non-stop seven days a week, ten hours a day, for the last six months while developing and coordinating all aspects of the classic musical. With the support of her production assistant, Donna, she feels secure and confident the stage play will run smoothly, knowing everything will be in her diligent, capable hands.

She is thankful the warm summer weather is cooperating today with clear skies and not a storm cloud in sight from Milwaukee to Indianapolis. She lugs and bounces her dust-covered golf clubs up from the basement and drags them through the apartment, propping them up in the front hall while listening and not wanting to miss the call from Andrew as to when he will be picking her up.

Andrew is a well-known personal injury attorney at the prestigious Chambers Law Firm located on Randolph Street in downtown Chicago, which his father established in 1980, and both he and his sister Ashley are now partners.

Amy is aware of his pivotal 10 AM meeting today with a potentially lucrative client, an elderly disabled widow, who was hit and run over by a Harlem Avenue bus on her way to Sunday morning Mass at St. Monica's Church. The case is a no-brainer and could easily reward the plaintiff ten million plus dollars from the defendant, The Chicago Transit Authority, while the Chambers Law Firm's take at 33% would be oh so sweet. However, his plans to meet Amy for their one o'clock tee time at the Sydney Marovitz Golf Course, with its spectacular view of the beautiful lakefront, the same course the old timers still call Waveland Golf Course, looks dimmer and dimmer by the minute.

At noon, he calls disappointed he has to cancel their golf date but ecstatic that the elderly grandmother has agreed for him to represent her. Her reason and logic: he reminds her of her youngest and favorite grandson. Feeling this called for celebration, he and his sister invited her to accompany them to Gibson's Steak House on Rush Street for lunch and afterward will ensure she is safely tucked away in an Uber on her way back home, avoiding the city's perils and risks.

Although the news lets her down, she also recognizes that she, more times than he, has canceled at the last minute due to her job. Teasing him, she laughs, saying all is good, noting she will just have to wait to beat his cute little ass another time, and both agree to meet later this evening to take a stroll to D'Agostinos Pizza & Pub on Southport Avenue for dinner tonight.

Back again to the basement, go the bouncing golf clubs. Eyeing her bike, thoughts cross her mind of a peaceful ride along the gorgeous lakefront until she remembers the bike trails that look so peaceful and serene in the Visit Chicago brochures are definitely not a place to relax. The congestion of Lake Shore Drive and the gobs of power walkers and professional cyclists killing for a spot on the trail, all wove together with the irritating loud city commotion and chaos, exploding in every direction, is definitely not conducive to relaxation.

She decides, instead, to hike to her favorite tranquil destination, the eerie historical Graceland Cemetery. Trekking north on Racine Avenue towards the graveyard, she avoids the chaotic excitement of Wrigley Field, where die-hard Cub fans have been gathering since early this morning in hopes their beloved Cubbies will clobber the antagonistic St. Louis Cardinals in today's game.

Even the thunderous echoes from Wrigley Field become somber and suppressed when traveling across the spooky cemetery built in 1860, which many Chicagoans believe to be haunted. Two thousand deep-rooted trees with monstrous outstretched limbs, many being weeping willow trees, smother any sunlight and project long shadows on the crumbling century-old tombs, where ghosts are rumored to hide, and some of the country's most hair-raising burial sites are located.

She turns her head downward and lowers her eyes, not wanting to look at the tall statue of the sinister, long hooded figure with his grim blackened face, known as "The Eternal Silence", also called "The Shadow of Death". It is believed if you stare and lock eyes with him, you will see a version of your own death.

She shudders seeing tourists approaching the statue, holding up their cameras and phones and snapping pictures of him, as it is rumored anyone doing so takes the chance of their camera malfunctioning or pictures being blurry, but even worse, awful unexpected events will happen to anyone attempting to take a photo.

The creepiest thing for Amy are the ancient headstones encased with large oval photographs of long-dead children, dressed in the fine clothing of the 1800s, staring out at you and seemingly begging for your help to escape and play with ordinary children.

With the many dead children buried in the cemetery, Inez Clarke is probably the most famous. Six-year-old Inez died in 1880 while on a picnic with her parents after being struck by lightning during a terrible thunderstorm and dying before their eyes. Wanting to keep her forever, they had a life-sized sculpture of her created while smiling and sitting on a wooden chair holding an umbrella and encased it in glass.

It is said that she grows frightened during thunderstorms, and the glass case can be found empty during such times as she wanders the cemetery trying to find her parents' grave site, which is located under a nearby sprawling tree with dangling wind chimes. Visitors still place gifts on the gravesite, and reports of wind chimes and a young girl crying are often made. Some even claim to have seen a young girl wearing an old-fashioned dress dancing through the graveyard.

Having gathered much of this history from Andrew, a member of the Chicago Historical Society and a Graceland history buff, and after taking many interesting and fascinating walks here over the years, she spots his family mausoleum peeking through the ominous weeping willow trees just ahead.

For a family that insists on the best of everything from Silver Oaks Napa Valley Cabernet Sauvignon to Porsche Cayenne automobiles to their wooded country estate in Door County, she is mystified that the Chambers family is so prideful of this crumbling, deteriorating monument, covered in a web of thick bug-infested vines clinging fiercely to the damp, moldy walls. Slumped in the middle of a jungle of overgrown bushes and clumps of weeds, the mausoleum cruelly sneers at her, furious that an intrusive outsider is trespassing and has no business being here.

The gruesome mausoleum seems to apprehend that she is approaching and demands silence, as the crickets stop chirping and the birds no longer sing but fly away in fear, with only her soft footsteps breaking the unnatural silence. Standing on tip-toe, peering through the open bars on the door, she recoils, inhaling the rancid smell of death and decay. Sensing the fine hairs on her arms rise, she feels an immediate temperature drop, chilling her to the bone and leaving her with a disturbing feeling of dread.

An unexplained urge to enter the mausoleum overcomes her as if a sinister apparition is inviting her in. As her eyes grow blurry, the crypt lowest to the bottom appears to be cracked open. Amy gasps, spotting the aggressive Norway rats huddling next to it while one lifting his head seems to sense her but then returns to using his sharp teeth to continue gnawing out a burrow large enough for an army of long-tailed rats to squeeze their enormous bodies through.

The powerful blow to the back of her head erupts in a blinding flash before her eyes, and an explosion of excruciating pain as she falls to the ground, stunned by the attack. Never losing consciousness but feeling thick blood oozing down both sides of her face, her quivering hands struggle to wipe away the blood flooding her eyes and mouth.

Dazed and trembling, she winces as she grabs the razor-sharp pine needles on a low-hanging spruce tree while trying to support herself as she struggles to stand up. On her feet, she staggers through the bushes, reaching the pathway, only to encounter one of the popular cemetery walking tours in progress. The tour guide is providing a well-practiced historical and frightening narration of the graveyard, causing the group to already be on edge when she stumbles and falls in front of them, causing the group to break out in hysteria.

With screams and gasps of horror from the devoted horror fans and gales of laughter from others in the group, presuming it is just part of an act, a concerned doctor in the crowd, fearing the worst, examines her while his voice booms for someone to call 911.

Along with the speedy arrival of the paramedics, the doctor still shouting orders and the irksome lookie-loos, the curious crowd continues to grow, ignoring the elderly, distraught Filipino woman, who has been crying and praying over the adjacent freshly dug grave. Clutching her face and shaking her head in frustration, all could hear her panic-stricken screams of "babae, babae" over and over. Everyone feeling her sorrow for what they presumed must be the tragic loss of her baby grandchild, respectfully turn a blind eye, leaving her alone with her grief and anguish.

However, things may have been different if any one of the by-standers was fluent in the Philippine language of Tagalog because the word "babae" she was screaming, sounding like the broken English version of baby, was the Tagalog word for woman, the woman she saw hunched down and hiding behind the huge marble gravestone.

****

Not even the thickest stage make-up could hide and conceal her puffy black eye and swollen face, but Amy felt two days was enough time off, and she was itching to get back to work. Hearing the frustration in Donna's voice, advising her the awesome musical director had just up and left for New York with a better job offer in hand, and Poppy becoming more patronizing and less dependable than ever, she dismissed Andrew's pleas to stay home and drove through the rain to the theatre.

Trying not to dwell on the attack, but still so fresh in her mind, she has little confidence whoever did this to her will be caught. The police have as much told her so, explaining by the time the police officers burst through the cemetery gates with their blue lights flashing, the perpetrator was likely long gone. The young cop had tried to assure her it was no doubt a mentally ill homeless person who had already fled and disappeared into the crowd of noisy Cub fans clogging busy Clark Street, having no recollection of what he did.

The one-page official police report, taken at the Town Hall District 19 Police station, had probably already been forgotten as being a low priority, especially since her assault was the same day the carjacking of a Fire Department Battalion Chief's beloved Mercedes Benz occurred behind the popular Bernie's Tap and Grill across from Wrigley Field.

The heavenly fragrance from the stunning vase of gorgeous lilacs and white calla lilies, along with the gigantic card signed by the entire troupe, was first to welcome her as she stepped into her office. They would not only be the best reason but the only good reason to be back at work today.

She has not even finished reading the verse in the card when Donna abruptly walks in and immediately shuts the door, and she suspects this must be something serious. Donna is visibly frustrated and pissed off and goes into a tirade about Poppy's sudden obnoxious ego, which has grown to epic proportions since receiving a strong favorable review in the Chicago Sun-Times and has gone so far as demanding Donna locate and purchase additional copies of the article for her.

Hoping to keep the peace, Amy attempts to settle her down, promising she will immediately have a word with Poppy while agreeing the request was unacceptable and demeaning. Praising her for her professionalism, excellent character and strong work ethic, she acknowledges she is the glue that holds the production company together, promising to reward her, especially for taking on all of the additional painstaking responsibilities. She is shaken by Donna's sharp tongue when she hurls the words at her that "talk and promises are cheap" while reminding her having already lost one key member of the crew, it might be time to start worrying about losing another one.

The hopes of having a peaceful first day back to work have long disappeared, and owing it to Donna for being the exceptional employee she has proven to be, she decides to immediately complete and forward the necessary paperwork to Corporate requesting an Exemplary Employee Bonus, which she so well deserves.

All forms, including the company personnel files, are locked in the top drawer of the metal file cabinet, boldly marked Confidential in Amy's office. Before inserting the key, she is alarmed, seeing the wild flurry of scratches around the keyhole and fears that someone has tried to pry it open. When she drags out the hefty drawer, discovering misfiled folders and papers askew, it is evident that the private files have been rifled through.

Horrified, she checks her own file first to determine if the disturbing letter sent from September is still where she carefully hid it after folding it in quarters and burying it deep in the middle of her Blue Cross & Blue Shield insurance forms. With her heart pounding, she thankfully finds the letter safely hidden. But was it safely hidden away, or what she fears most, did someone read it?

****

Never losing her German accent, since relocating to the United States over sixty years ago, Anna repeats her exacting instructions: the ficus tree needs to be watered only on Thursdays, the African violets every three days, the spider plant only on Mondays and continues while Amy hurriedly scribbles the directions onto the note pad.

Amy's wonderful grandmotherly and grandfatherly tenants, Anna and Joseph Heiser, have entrusted her to take care of their plants, which saturate their old-fashioned second-floor apartment. No better tenants could she be gifted with, as the elderly retired couple are quiet, assist with the maintenance of the building and always keep a watchful eye on the house.

Having sold their apartment building on Aldine Avenue five years ago, as they could no longer maintain the six apartments to their high standards, they did not want to leave the neighborhood. Amy, a single woman investing her life's worth in a two-flat in the city, who knew nothing about the upkeep of a building but loved the neighborhood, blessed the day they had struck up a conversation at the annual Flower & Garden Show at Navy Pier bringing about a perfect solution for all.

An anxious Anna, hovering over Joseph, double checking if he has the printed boarding passes and his passport, is stressing out both he and Amy now that the long-awaited day has finally arrived. The delighted couple are returning to their roots in charming Heidelberg, Germany, for a long-anticipated vacation and reunion with remaining family and old friends. Not wanting the added stress brought on them by waiting for a taxi or Uber, Amy has volunteered to drive them to the airport. With roly-poly Anna finally plopping down in the car's front seat, Amy hands her the sturdy cane and closes the door.

Amy's little Honda is loaded down with their fifty-year-old, well-traveled red Samsonite luggage, which is more durable and heavier than any made today, as she speeds along the Kennedy Express heading to International Terminal 5 at Chicago O'Hare Airport. At the same time, Anna continues to rattle off a list of things she may have forgotten to do, i.e., did she unplug the

Mr. Coffee Maker, did she pack her bi-focal glasses, but most concerning, did she lock the back door? Amy assures her she most likely did lock it, being as cautious as she is but will check so immediately upon returning home, and this seems to satisfy the nervous Anna.

By the time she arrives back home, it is well after eight o'clock in the evening, and the city's warm-colored LED street lights have turned on. Gazing at her dark, unlit house, a sudden moment of panic grips Amy, and she wonders if the Heisers forgot to set the light timers she recently purchased at Ace Hardware for their trip.

Typically, looking up at the second floor after dark, she would see cheery light shining through the three front windows, capturing the beauty of the kaleidoscope of brilliant colors in the stained glass window hangings, each depicting a group of beautiful songbirds. However, tonight, with no moonlight and the sky heavy with dark clouds, the building she loves so much suddenly appears sinister, taking the form of a huge, intimidating stranger, and for the first time, she is frightened to enter the house.

After grabbing an ice-cold Pepsi from the fridge, her hand can't reach into the greasy Portillo's bag quickly enough, not having eaten since breakfast, and she decides to break her promise to Anna of going upstairs first thing to inspect the Mr. Coffee Maker and check the potentially unlocked back door.

Eating and savoring every bite of the juicy Italian beef sandwich and leaving only a few fries, she quickly picks up the wrappers and used napkins tossing them into the stainless trash can. She slips into her favorite pair of moccasins, grabs her tiny pen flashlight from the junk drawer and proceeds to climb the twisting back stairs, surprised at how cool and dark it is outside.

Knowing she only needs the flashlight for the first flight of porch stairs, she is momentarily startled and becomes nervous when Joseph's motion sensor system doesn't kick in, flooding the porch with its blinding light. Tense and hesitant, she stands perfectly still with the growing sensation she is not alone on the open-air porch. With her hands trembling, the shaky beam from the flashlight weaves in and out, slowly investigating the row of leafy potted plants ending in the corner by the lush potted Japanese maple tree as a voice inside her impulsively screams for her to turn and run.

She is only an arms-length away from confirming if the worrisome back door is open, and like wildfire, she swiftly reaches over, twisting the knob, and finds it securely locked. Relief instantly floods over her, and she drops her guard, but just as suddenly, a slight movement from the potted tree in the corner catches her eye. A horrifying scream, starting slow and barreling to a crescendo, rips from her throat, seeing the low-hanging branches slowly being pushed to the side as a grotesque hooded figure emerges.

Clad in the same floor-length cape, with the draping hood concealing his dark, shrouded face, the horrifying figure is almost identical to the eerie, legendary Statue of Death from Graceland Cemetery. His blazing, unholy red eyes leer angrily out from under the hood, burning into Amy as her screams intensify.

With a powerful slap from the back of his hand, her head ricochets left, with blood spewing on him from her deeply split lip. Fearing for her life, she feels his thick, calloused fingers choke her throat and painfully rip the delicate necklace from her neck. Stunned and lying on the cold linoleum, she listens to bizarre chanting rambling from a shrill, high-pitched voice as he slowly descends the shadowy back stairs.

Several worried neighbors, hearing the blood-curdling screams, resulted in numerous calls being made to 911. Shivering, with her bruised face stuck to her own sticky blood pooling on the floor, she is thankful to hear the paramedic's heavy boots stomping up the wooden stairs and crossing over the porch while her painful lip throbs to the beat of the wailing police siren growing closer.

Placing an IV in her limp arm, the freckle-faced paramedic assures her she is doing great. Now strapped onto the stretcher cart being transported down the steep stairs, and with each bang from the wheels hitting a step, she winces, fighting to hold back any more tears.

After receiving the call from an emergency room nurse, a shaken Andrew abruptly ends his workout at the prominent East Bank Club. His sweaty, muscular body storms through the locker room, grabbing only his gym bag, and without changing into street clothes, he recklessly blows through stop lights, racing to Illinois Masonic Hospital.

While being led through the loud, chaotic corridor of the emergency room, he hears the gagging sounds from the grubby wino and jumps back just as vomit shoots out in front of him. Overflowing with kids howling and crying for their mothers and a sea of old people moaning with fractured bones and bandaged head wounds, the nurse finally pulls back the curtain of Amy's cubicle. Her dark, tangled hair is sticking up wildly and still in the same blood-stained sweatshirt, she is struggling to hold the freezing ice pack to her lip.

Spotting Andrew, she immediately bursts into tears and pleads for him to take her home. The gruesome attack has more damaging mental consequences than her bruised mouth and split lip, and the compassionate, overworked emergency room doc agrees to release her with Andrew's promise to stay the night and care for her.

Back home hours later, lying in her bed, she sleeps soundly under the lilac-flowered duvet after being heavily sedated. However, Andrew is wide awake and restless, constantly turning from side to side and unable to sleep.

At 2 AM, he hears the toxic honking of a car out front. Trudging across the living room floor and peeking out from behind the curtains, he spots what he believes might be an Uber parked out front. The honking kicks in again as the driver starts laying on the horn for an even longer length of time.

Pissed and adrenalin surging through his system, he charges out to the vehicle, raising his fist high and slamming it down violently on the hood. The elderly Uber driver is visibly shaken and keeps repeating he is so sorry while confessing he knew this gig was too good to be true.

Andrew is livid and demands an explanation from the remorseful senior citizen. He explains that a woman contacted him at midnight, offering an insane amount of money to pick up a fare at this address promptly at 2 AM with strict instructions to remain in the car and not approach the door. He was to honk when he arrived, and she stated the party would be waiting and ready to be picked up precisely at that time.

Considering it odd, he surmised the fare was an individual who had drunk too much, not wishing to be perceived as requiring assistance while walking to the auto, or possibly, the prank of some crazy Pi Kappa Alpha frat boys from Loyola University perpetrated on some naive freshman. However, when two hundred dollars was transferred to his account, and it was such a short trip, he was ecstatic for his good fortune. When no one appeared, he grew fearful of angering the neighbors when observing lights popping on in darkened apartment windows but didn't know what to do.

Feeling sympathy for the poor old guy, Andrew assures him he is in no trouble, and since no one at this address had ordered the Uber, he suggests he just return home. However, he poses one more question, curious about the ride's destination. Embarrassed, the old man sheepishly lowers his eyes and whispers 4001 N. Clark Street, Graceland Cemetery.

CHRISTINE

Carefully parking her shiny, black Audi next to the dented white Ford 150 pickup truck with "Joseph Lombardo & Sons" scrawled across its side, she cringes, realizing it cannot be good news if it is still parked under the huge, shady oak tree.

Deliberately avoiding the slow stream of water spilling out from the bathroom and trickling down the hall floor, she reaches into the linen closet to grab a few towels to soak it up before further damage can be done to the pristine, hardwood floors.

Sticking her head into the boys' bathroom to survey the damage, she grimaces, seeing the toilet lying sideways on the floor surrounded by sopping wet towels and the dreaded snake machine. Jumping when she hears Cookie yell a loud "Gotcha", the plumber victoriously raises her arm, waving the retrieved red Hot Wheel car over her head. Cookie is Joe Lombardo's daughter who, along with Joey Jr. and Joseph Sr., are the most sought-after team of residential plumbers in Lake County.

Christine, perched on the bathtub watching her meticulously reassemble the toilet, asks the plumber how her dad is, knowing he is recovering from triple bypass surgery. Cookie groans as she tightens the anchor bolts onto the floor and laughs, saying he is doing terrific and itching to be back at work bossing her and her brother around. She shares that Joey has taken over most of the business, and she is only working part-time, helping out on minor jobs and emergency calls since giving birth to her two little girls, now three and four years old.

Bam! The back door slams shut, and she hears an ear-deafening yell with Mark screaming his bloody head off and Tammy following close behind, struggling to keep up with him. Clutching the fingers on his right hand, he throws himself into his mother's arms, and observing they are already turning purple, she brings them to her lips and gently kisses them.

With tears pouring down his face, he points at Tammy, blaming her while shouting it is all her fault and that she did it on purpose. Tammy, nearly in tears herself, explains she had no idea he was behind her when she accidentally shut the screen door on his fingers and apologizes profusely. At the same time, he keeps insisting she did it on purpose and wants to kill him. Christine knows her son so well, and with way too much television, a teasing older brother and Mark's overactive imagination, it doesn't surprise her that he constantly believes someone is trying to kill him.

"Hey, Markie, can you give me a hand here and help me tighten these bolts," Cookie asks. Dropping to his knees, she lets him turn the adjustable pipe wrench, and there is no more mention of Tammy, the finger killer. The two mothers shrug their shoulders and smile as the child now allows Tammy to ice his sore fingers.

Beginning this morning with the reunion of the Alphabet Girls, the flooded upstairs floor forged by the nose-diving Hot Wheel toy car, and topping it off with Markie's meltdown, Christine knows tonight will definitely be a pizza night. Inviting Tammy to stay and accepting her offer to help get the boys ready for bed, she realizes she still has not heard from her husband.

Rinsing the sweet-smelling conditioner from her hair, finally having time for herself after listening to the kids' prayers and tucking them in for the night, she hears the sharp chirping from her cell phone. Tumbling from the shower and not even toweling off, she races wet and naked to seize the phone from her pillow. She frustratingly slams the phone on her bed, silently screaming when she misses Charles' call, and waits until the voicemail symbol pops up to hear his message.

She listens to his enthusiastic, velvety voice droning on about how he successfully procured additional government funding for the foundation. He apologizes for the briefness of the message, explaining he is just now heading out for a late-night dinner at Mastro's Steakhouse, joined by two pivotal East Coast senators to celebrate the victory. He abruptly ends with a half-hearted "Love you".

Hopeful he may pick up when she instantly returns the call, she is deeply disappointed when her call goes immediately to voice mail. Thinking 10:30 PM was a hell of a time for dinner, she remembers his Executive Assistant, Dana Rae, gushing about this restaurant not too long ago, and she leaves a sadly disappointed message of "Love you too".

****

"And let's not forget, if our Illinois corn wants to be knee-high by the fourth of July, our farmers will be thankful for this much-needed rain," beams the giddy WGN weather girl, and thus, the wailing begins.

Rain surging down from the gloomy sky violently pelts the windows, and with the booming unexpected crack of thunder above, John jumps back and clutches his blanket even tighter. The Midwest downpour shows no sign of letting up, and the four glum brothers are devastated that their long-awaited trip to fun-packed Great America won't be happening today. No Roaring River, no Sprocket Rockets and no Dark Knight.

She called Tammy earlier, notifying her she was canceling the trip, and she now has to deal with four disappointed, rambunctious boys who will be cooped up inside the house for the entire day. She hopes and prays that Charles' flight will land on time and he will return home by noon as there are not enough Disney movies, video games or crafts in the world to make this day more bearable.

By four o'clock, it's two-year-old John's choice of a game, and, of course, he comes running out of his bedroom clinging to the beat-up Cootie game. The game barely surviving three older brothers has missing eyes, broken antennae and legs no longer able to support poor Cootie and still no Charles.

Hearing the ping from her phone of an incoming text, just as Luke yelps with joy, completing his cootie first, and John bursts out in tears losing the game, she dives at her phone. It reads: "Trying all day to contact you, prob with your phone? Flight still delayed, no further info" followed by a string of yellow sad-faced emojis.

Lightning bolts continue to bombard the stormy sky, while thunder continues to bellow and rumble for miles as the summer storm continues to rage with no chance of ending soon. Her husband is stuck in DC, and with bedtime coming quickly and no sign of the children tiring, she has no choice but to relent and let her sons build a tent in the great room and camp out in it overnight. After hauling up the card tables and covering them in tattered old blankets, the excited children are all camped out, chowing down on hot dogs and potato chips, while she digs through their closets searching for their Chicago Blackhawks and White Sox sleeping bags.

At ten o'clock, she peeks into the tents and finds everyone sound asleep while squashed together and snuggling their stuffed animals. She smiles, taking in Luke, much like herself as a child, who cuddles with his favorite Georgie, the giraffe.

Not wanting to sleep upstairs and leave the children alone for the night, she props herself up on the white shag pillow resting on the black leather couch and flicks on the fifty-inch Sony television to catch Kate Winslet in the romantic movie *The Reader*. Keeping the volume turned off, she squints to read the subtitles for fear of waking the children.

The new house is gigantic, sitting in the middle of five acres of woodlands with an attached four-car garage, expansive attic, chilled wine cellar, fully equipped home gymnasium and sauna on the lower level. Yet, it produces as many frightening and ghostly noises in the middle of the night as an old eerie 1890s farmhouse.

The ear-deafening blast of thunder shakes her from a light

sleep, and springing from the couch while still disoriented, she prowls the house, ensuring all the deadbolts are firmly in place and hoping that she hasn't forgotten to set the security alarm again.

She would have thought, with Charles traveling so much and being away from home so often, she would be used to it by now, and quite honestly, she is. However, being alone in this enormous house, with only the kids, on the night a violent thunderstorm has savagely rolled in from Wisconsin, she is frightened and tense with her nerves on edge.

Uneasy and spooked by the storm, she stares out the great room's vast ceiling-to-floor windows, gazing at the magnificent oak trees swaying wildly in the violent wind, struggling to stay upright. The sorrowful weeping willow trees are arched and bowed over while their huge bent branches angrily sweep the ground, and the howling wind seems to roar even louder.

The epic cathedral ceilings, partnered with the lightning strikes darting through the glass windows and the ominous glow of the television, have created long, disturbing shadows on the twelve-foot-high walls, appearing to be deep cracks and fissures. Her imagination growing, she envisions heinous beasts, long trapped behind the walls, savagely fighting to escape. Using razor-sharp talons to rip open the wallboard and finally burst free, they slither down the walls to hunt down and devour her and the children.

Hearing the swing banging against the railing on the porch, she peers out the window at the exact moment a bolt of lightning engulfs the porch with light. She is terrorized by observing what she believes to be a lone woman encountering torrential rain pouring down on her while huddled near the swing. Frozen and unable to move, another bolt of lightning strikes seconds later, and the ghostly apparition has disappeared.

Minutes pass, and unable to control her erratic breathing, she is scared to death and terrified for her family's safety. Numb with fear, her eyes target the porch once more, and she is startled when she hears slow-moving footsteps echoed by the sudden muffled knocking on the front door.

The unexpected, ear-piercing blast from the alarm has the sleepy, frightened boys racing out from under their tent and scurrying into her waiting arms as she stands rigid, unable to imagine what savagery is about to happen to her family. With the children crying and yelling, the alarm blaring and her heart beating double-time, she prays they survive until the Lake Zurich police arrive.

Hearing the wailing sirens abruptly stop out front and seeing blue lights bouncing off the window, she realizes the police have arrived but also regretfully understands the intruder is probably long gone. Yet, she's incorrect because all five of them, gaping out the window, see the two beefy police officers cuff and brutally thrust an individual onto the muddy ground. He is furious and swearing obscenities at the top of his lungs, and she gasps, knowing why, because this is his house, it's Charles.

Exasperated, he explains that O'Hare International Airport finally gave the all-clear for DC flights to land in Chicago after midnight, and his packed American Airlines flight landed at 1 AM. Taking a limo home and traveling down the winding driveway, he was stunned viewing the damage the wind had wrought on their grounds, and in his hurry to enter the house, he forgot his phone on the backseat of the Cadillac XTS.

Fearing he would alarm her, arriving at this late hour, he thought it best he knock on the door, and when his knock went unanswered, he surmised she was sound asleep. When he entered the house, he heard a swooshing sound causing him to spin around and witness one of the magnificent oak trees being uprooted and crashing to the ground, leaving no time to reach the security system keypad and enter the code.

The kids are finally settled and asleep after being pumped up from the exciting double adventure of the terrifying storm and the police pummeling their dad to the ground. While Christine sips from a cup of calming green tea and Charles from a large crystal glass filled with one-hundred-proof Irish whiskey, they console each other and enjoy the peacefulness after surviving the harrowing night.

Charles assures her that although a few trees were lost, the landscaper can easily replant healthy, young saplings, and the most important thing is that no one in the family was hurt or injured. However, no matter how soothing or reassuring his voice is, he cannot persuade her to turn away from the conversation and forget about the strange woman she believes she saw on the porch.

Grasping her hands in his, he tries to convince her that most burglars or criminals would not be foolish enough to venture out in a life-threatening storm like this, joking that even criminals have some common sense.

Regarding the mysterious woman she presumes to have seen, he begs her to look seriously at the circumstances and view them logically. He poses the question, "Why would a crazy woman go out on a tumultuous night like this, trudging up a random driveway while fighting the ferocious winds and torrential rain pelting down on her, only to hide on a porch?"

She is thinking about it, and there is no doubt in her mind that an insane, diabolical woman would most definitely plow through the dreadful storm, eagerly anticipating the perfect environment to sadistically and brutally murder the birth mother she hates.

****

When you have four little boys, sleeping late is never penciled in on your day planner; most family and friends know that. So when Charles' phone rings at 7 AM the following morning, he is not concerned seeing the incoming call from Dana Rae, his meticulous and selfless executive assistant. After not receiving his promised call to do so, she is calling to inquire if he made it home safely last night.

While Christine is filling his glass with orange juice, she hears a string of uh huh, uh huh, uh huh and finally, of course, she wouldn't forget. Laying his phone down and reaching for the jar of raspberry jam, he says, "You didn't forget this Friday, did you?" This was the day The Boys & Girls Club of Chicago's annual black-tie fundraiser and silent auction was being held and attended by Chicago's most influential movers and shakers, from union presidents to big-shot politicians to local entertainers, which was being held at the landmark Shedd Aquarium located on the beautiful Chicago lakefront.

"Really, Charles? With Dana Rae's daily reminders, do you really think it would just slip my mind?" she irritatingly asks. "Your Brioni tux has been back from Enzo's for a week now, perfectly cleaned and pressed and safely hanging just where you like it on the left side of your walk-in closet."

Unlike most couples, she spends more time getting Charles prepared and dressed for a special event than herself. She knows she will decide at the last minute which of the ordinary outfits now lining her closet to wear, never seeing the need to impress at these extravaganzas as so many patrons of the arts do, especially the women. Charles is on the Board of Directors and is expected to make an appearance, and usually a grand one at that. She wonders how many of the benefactors have questioned why the effervescent Charles has such an ordinary wife.

With Charles outside surveying the damage from the storm last night and the boys going berserk while playing and hiding from him under the fallen limbs, she loads the dishwasher while watching the *Live with Kelly and Ryan* talk show, featuring everyday housewives before and after make-overs. She is stunned by how the make-up artists, stylists, and fashion consultants, in less than an hour, have transformed these average, ordinary-looking women into beauties and wonders if Charles sees her in the before category.

He is always loving and attentive, and although aware his handsome good looks do not go unnoticed by other women, she has never been insecure in their marriage. However, she does sense something off with him lately with his failing to answer her phone calls or their going directly to voicemail, plus the growing number of hours and days he spends away from home.

Following the event in 1992, she has always downplayed her stunning good looks, never wanting to attract unwanted attention from the opposite sex. But seeing the excitement in the made-over housewives' eyes, she has an epiphany and decides to amaze Charles by having a makeover herself. She plans to premier this brand new version of herself Friday at the ritzy fundraiser in front of zebra sharks, porcupine fish and brightly colored mandarin dragonets sashaying and whisking around the Wild Reef exhibit.

Having Tammy on speed dial, and with fingers crossed, she hopes she is available to babysit today, being it is so last minute. A groggy Tammy answers the phone, and hearing a masculine teasing laugh in the background, she realizes she is not alone. Christine pleads with Tammy and coerces her to come over as soon as possible, only after the enticement of an additional two hundred dollars, adding it should be an effortless day as Charles is home and is packing up the kids and taking them for a bike ride after John wakes from his nap.

She is more than a babysitter, but that's what Christine has always called her, embarrassed to tell people she has an au pair or nanny. They met before the kids were born while she sweated through Tammy's strenuous aerobics class at LA Fitness, and the two slowly became friends.

Christine, not having any real friends but a good grip on life, and Tammy, a scatterbrained extrovert, not knowing where tomorrow would lead, bonded over leg lifts and jumping jacks while bouncing to the energetic beats of 1960s rock and roll. Tammy, twenty years old at the time, was mentored by Christine, and valuing her sage advice, returned to community college and, at a snail's pace, eventually received her associate's degree. Still taking online college courses after ten years, she is now only six credits away from achieving her long-sought bachelor's degree.

Although impulsive and carefree, she has always proven to be responsible, and the kids love her as she would rather play dodgeball with them than remind them to start their homework. Working forty-plus hours a week for the family, although her hours vary from hour to hour and day to day, she is very well paid yet always seems short of cash and is forever asking Christine for an advance on her salary.

An hour later, Christine, donning her mom jeans, punches Northbrook Court into her GPS and heads towards I-94 East, making her way to Neiman Marcus.

Trusting nothing to herself, she seeks out professional advice from the store's private stylist, Manuel, explaining she needs his fashionable expertise in selecting a fabulous gown to wear to the swank charity affair. Gushing over her, he is thrilled, insisting he has the most amazing dress for her flawless size two body – a sensual Carolina Herrera strapless, two-tone, gold metallic evening gown. Giggling like a schoolgirl, she fawns over the Dolce & Gabanna metallic ankle-strap sandals while his manicured hands clasp the brilliant platinum Lana six-strand choker necklace and magnificent matching drop earring and holds them up to the light.

Having a difficult time holding back his exuberance, he excitedly reaches out to his personal friend Lanie Kiko, the Chicago celebrity hair and make-up artist, via a Zoom call to consult with the two of them.

Requesting Christine tilt her face left and right, then lift her nose to the sky, Lanie raves about her delicate bone structure and high fashion cheekbones, confessing he would love to do her hair and make-up for the upcoming gala. With his hands madly skipping across the screen, he suggests what he, as a board-certified colorist, would do with her brown medium-length hair. He romanticizes a creamy light honey blonde color that draws attention to her arctic blue eyes and flawless complexion, and he would create a chic high-volume updo piled up with layers of curls and twists into a look of pure elegance.

Returning home and turning down the driveway, she spots the bicycle brigade having broken down, with bikes sprawled on the road and one lying at the bottom of the overgrown ditch. Charles is shouting orders while trying to balance baby John on the rear bicycle seat, who only now begins to cry seeing his mother, while the other brothers are bobbing up and down trying to look after and console Markie.

There is always one in every family, and Markie is theirs. He is the kid that will fall off the pier, get the fishing hook caught in his finger, swallow sand while swimming, or what looks like what happened today, lose control of his bike while trying to pass his older brother.

Steering the car to the side of the road, she jumps out, darting to baby John and unsnapping him from the infant seat, lifts him into her arms while Charles drops the bike to the ground and races to Markie. With a deep gash in his knee, covered with dirt and blood oozing out, the kid is screaming bloody murder.

Charles picks him up and comforts him while he once again claims someone is trying to kill him. Eyeing each other, Christine and Charles try not to laugh, hearing his customary explanation for every mishap.

Plopping baby John and Markie back in the car, she drives back to the house while the other two boys and Charles brainstorm on how to return all the bikes to the yard.

Tammy is waiting on the porch steps, having heard all the commotion, and grabs the baby from Christine's arms as she whisks Markie to the bathroom to hunt for the Bactine to clean his wound and survey the damage.

With the others returning, Charles enters the bathroom to a much quieter version of Markie, just in time to help put the final Sponge Bob bandage across his knee. The entire family have now crowded into the bathroom and cheer when Tammy appears with popsicles but begin fighting over who gets the final grape one as they traipse after her down the hall.

Tugging at her sleeve, Charles holds Christine back from joining the parade and has a troubled expression on his face. He admits he is no handyman but warns her after inspecting Markie's bicycle; it is evident the chain has been tampered with and partially sawn through, which no doubt caused his accident.

He is adamant that whatever caused this required some strength and insists it could not possibly have been the boys, even if they had tried.

****

Christine keeps a watchful eye on the speedometer, hoping the cop who needs to meet his monthly quota of tickets is somewhere else resting his arm out the open patrol car window.

With the late afternoon sun starting to slowly descend, it blinds her freshly made-up eyes as she pulls up to the house and parks the Audi. Spotting Tammy and the kids setting up empty mason jars and punching holes into the lids, she smiles, knowing they are counting down the hours till dark, preparing for their long-anticipated hunt to catch and collect fireflies and stay up well past their bedtimes.

Exactly one hour later, Charles' phone pings with a text from the limo driver, advising he has arrived and is waiting out front. Growing concerned after Christine banned him from seeing her until it was time to depart and aware she is always ready well before him, his jaw drops seeing her descend the winding staircase. She is dazzling and an absolute knockout!

The man with the smoky, sexy voice who is always so articulate and eloquent is speechless, barely recognizing this stunning woman as his wife. With newfound confidence, she glides down the stairs to join him. She quickly turns her head to avoid smearing the perfectly applied Tom Ford Forbidden Pink lipstick, denying his vigorous attempt to deliver an unexpected, spontaneous kiss. Drawing her closely while encircling his muscular arms around her, he whispers in her ear, confessing he has never seen her look more beautiful. He offers her his arm, and she joins him while they step out into the warm summer night as though they are Chicago's very own royalty.

Lifting her gown delicately, she and Charles climb the high formal staircase of the John G. Shedd Aquarium, located on the picturesque Chicago lakefront. They marvel in awe as they walk through the towering Doric columns, hearing the romantic musical instrumental *The Way You Are* being performed by the forty-piece orchestra as they gracefully cascade through the open doors. This song is one of Christine's favorites, and she is reminded of the sweet and tender lyrics sung perfectly by Bruno Mars, which revolve around helping an insecure partner see her own beauty, a woman so much like herself.

The electrifying Caribbean Reef Exhibit, with its high translucent ceiling and dynamic overhead lighting, which caps the 5,800 square foot rotunda, is centered in the middle of the area. Showcasing sharks, stingrays, sea turtles and sparking yellow, flickering turquoise and blazing red angel fish that glide and swim about the massive circular tank, the museum has miraculously been transformed into an elegant ballroom.

Luxurious white linen table coverings, softly draping to the floor, are set perfectly with gold-trimmed white porcelain dinnerware, heavy crystal goblets, and wildly romantic floral arrangements of delicate yellow roses, fragrant purple calla lilies and flowering sweet peas.

An impressive stage for the orchestra and opulent dance floor has been painstakingly assembled at the east end of the ornate room. The energetic rhythm sections from The Chicago Timbre Band are coaxing hips to swing as the guests pick up the pulsating beat of Lady Gaga's *Stupid Love* and men with black bow ties and women in glittery gowns sashay toward the dance floor.

As the band succeeds in ushering the lively crowd into a euphoric mood, the harried wait staff continue to dodge exuberant guests who are sipping exotic cocktails while they balance and serve miniature beef Wellington, seared scallops and Japanese fried dumplings on silver platters.

Entering the ballroom, eyes drift toward the beautiful, sensual couple. There is never a lack of attention for Charles, a striking black man, standing at 6'4" with piercing amber eyes that play off his dark expresso skin, who looks so much like Denzel in his stylish Italian tuxedo. Still, all eyes tonight are on the breathtaking Christine. Walking arm in arm across the floor to their table, conversations stop and eyes gape at the gorgeous couple.

Dana Rae, abruptly appearing from nowhere, dressed in a lovely ocean blue lace gown with cap sleeves, rushes toward her boss and provides him cue cards to assist when giving his welcome speech and introducing the city dignitaries. Offering her customary artificial smile to Christine, attempting to cover her hidden disdain for her, she is clearly displeased and unable to hide her shock, noting her new appearance.

Never feeling included and always ignored, especially during past formal affairs, she is speechless when the city police commissioner, who is a notorious womanizer and narcissist, switches place cards with the newly appointed fire commissioner and sits down next to her. He pulls his chair a tad too close while striking up a conversation, and she can't decide what he is enjoying more, ogling her breasts or listening to the sound of his own voice. Relieved to be interrupted by the well-known Gold Coast alderwoman, she is flattered and stunned when she invites her to attend the opening of the captivating Van Gogh Exhibit at the Germania Club being held in her ward next week.

Following his inspiring welcome speech and heartfelt pitch for donations to the Boys & Girls Club of Chicago, Charles shares a hysterical story about the mayor as a child, and with the audience doubled over in laughter, he welcomes her honor to the podium.

After sitting back down next to his wife, he reaches under the table and holds her hand, hoping the mayor keeps her speech short as he is famished and is anxiously waiting for the marinated Chilean sea bass to be served.

When the arm-bending, politicking and schmoozing with all the correct people winds down, the socialites and partygoers break loose and storm the dance floor to the booming sounds of rock and roll.

Dancing, which was forbidden to Christine as a child and totally ending after the event, feels conspicuous sitting and watching everyone having fun. Wondering what Charles is doing as he approaches the band leader and whispers in his ear, she knows minutes later when AC/DC's raucous *You Shook Me All Night Long* ends, and the slow-moving melody of Roberta Flack's *The First Time Ever I Saw Your Face* sweeps over the dance floor. Reaching out for her hand, he guides her to the floor, where he holds her lovingly, and they sway in place to the beautiful musical adaptation with all eyes on them.

Both blissfully returning to their table, the police commissioner snatches her away from Charles and begins dragging her back to the dance floor for a rousing version of *The Twist*. Happy, relaxed and more confident from the chocolate martinis, she shrugs her shoulders and joins him, surprising herself when her body flashes back to long-forgotten moves.

With the limos beginning to line up in front of the aquarium and the guests saying their final goodbyes, she groans, feeling her sore aching feet. Having always worn comfortable low-heeled shoes, this is the first time she has experienced painful throbbing feet after a night of dancing in the gorgeous excruciating shoes, both too high and too tight, but she feels it has definitely been worth it.

She excuses herself from a conversation with Charles, the mayor and the police commissioner, feeling she needs to use the bathroom before the long ride home. Viewing the long line snaking out from the ladies' room, she questions a security guard if there are any additional restrooms, and he points and directs her to one further down the hall.

Calling out to her husband, she flashes him a just one-minute sign and points down the hall in the direction of the other bathroom, and he shakes his head in acknowledgment, knowing she may be a while.

At the first sound of the ear-piercing scream, the husky security guard takes off running. Followed quickly by the alert police commissioner and a horrified Charles, all three race in the direction of the terrifying cry. With his long strides, Charles easily passes the guard and the commissioner as he bolts first through the bathroom door. He gasps aloud, finding Christine with her body hunched over the blood-stained sink, gripping a handful of bloody paper towels while struggling to stop the blood from streaming down her face. He gags and winces at the sight of her razor-slashed face. The deep gash beginning at the top of her cheek and brutally ripping down her face has sliced entirely through the corner of her soft mouth.

BETH

Oddest breakfast of Beth's life. Silent with tears never seeming to end, Amy wept constantly while swiping and blowing her nose in the linen napkin and barely touched her breakfast. Christine never raised her eyes and just kept adding more and more syrup to her waffles, between gulping down at least five cups of coffee, while Sister Eleanor sympathized and suggested that the problem could probably be solved with prayer, asking if we all still used our rosary beads.

Climbing into her bruised 2009 Toyota Corolla beater, she clears the passenger seat by using her hand to briskly scrape the used Kleenex, crumpled Burger King wrappers and flurry of ashes that have missed and escaped the car's ashtray onto the filthy floor. Like most city workers, she gets back and forth to work driving a beater, a reliable old car that will not catch the eye of enterprising thieves wanting to either steal it or harvest its valuable catalytic convertor.

Not knowing how long the Alphabet Girl Meeting was going to last, she texts her best friend, Moira, confirming she will be able to make their three o'clock tee time at the idyllic Tam O'Shanter Golf Course in Niles and is defiant that the challenging par four first hole is not going to get the best of her today.

Both women have a passion for golf and are damn good at it. However, living on opposite sides of the city, they take turns dragging their clubs and playing at Tam on the north side and the Beverly Country Club on the south side, where Beth's father is still a member.

They literally butted heads the first time they met. Beth was a Might Mac from Mother McCauley High School and Moira was a Bandit from Resurrection High School. Beth vaulting high and wrestling down a rebound, swung around ferociously and slammed into Moira's face, breaking her nose during their senior year basketball playoff game. Although losing, Moira and Resurrection considered it a moral victory, losing by only ten points to the powerful all-girls Southside Catholic high school basketball team.

The duo has lots in common besides being best of friends with both standing five 5'10" tall in their stocking feet. Each is insanely competitive and almost always shoots par when golfing, both are proud Irish Catholics, and both being employed by the Chicago Police Department abide by their strict personal rule of refusing to date co-workers. And having a few differences, Beth likes Crunchy Taco Supremes from Taco Bell while Moira hates them, Beth roots for the White Sox while Moira cheers on the Cubs and Beth likes men and Moira likes women.

"Pay up Annika Sorenstam," teases Moira while holding out her hand and laughing, given that Beth owes her one buck today after losing to her on the ninth hole for the closest ball to the pin. Tossing their shoes and clubs in their respective cars, they adjust their sun visors and enter the Howard Street Inn for a Miller Lite, the best-loaded nachos in town and a large helping of eavesdropping.

Lots of retired cops play this course, and the two women always sit at a table close enough to eavesdrop on their loud hilarious tales and outlandish rumors regarding shenanigans by Chicago's Finest, past and present. They never tire of the cops hysterical back-in-the-day stories, political opinions, and what horse is running in the ninth race today at Hawthorne Race Track is a sure thing. The good old boys smile and toast them when they sit down, always referring to them as the girls, and never realizing they too are members of the same good old boys club.

On the drive back home, listening to all news radio station 780, Beth foresees and fears the savage summer months of Chicago when deadly murderous street gangs rev up recruitment by enticing unwanted twelve and thirteen-year-old kids with promises of fast, easy money.

The city has over 100,000 active gang members belonging to 60 gangs. The primary street gangs that pose the greatest threat are the Gangster Disciples, Black Disciples, Black P Stone Nation, Vice Lords and Latin Kings. These gangs have been active in Chicago for decades and are heavily involved in drug trafficking, extortion and murder, with gang warfare and retaliation being responsible for well over fifty percent of Chicago homicides.

Beth kicks herself for being the procrastinator she is and waiting until the last day to change the blue-striped sheets and pillowcases in the guest room, which have remained the same since her parents last visit. Thankfully, her house cleaner, Agnes, has performed her magic of scrubbing, dusting and polishing, preparing for their arrival and inspection of the home they once owned.

Driving up from Cape Corral, Florida to attend the elaborate fiftieth wedding celebration for Uncle Rich and Aunt Josephine, her parents plan on staying with her for a week or so. With their return, her worn beige La-Z-Boy should not be surprised to find itself dragged across the gouged hardwood floor and positioned smack in front of the picture window where her mother can return to old habits and keep watch on neighbors she no longer knows.

Fifteen years ago, her dad finally called it a day and retired after thirty years with the strenuous Chicago Police Department, and her folks packed up and drove south to oranges and sunnier days. Knowing she would need a Chicago address, as she planned to embark on a career in law enforcement with the city, her parents sold her the house she grew up in at the ridiculously low price only a parent would agree to.

Unlocking the door and entering the house, she gives it the

once over and sees that Danny has removed the last of his stuff. Feeling guilty for giving a really nice guy the boot, she's filled with guilt and regrets when she spots the only item he left behind.

Still sitting on top of the mahogany fireplace mantle is a framed photo of them looking deliriously happy. She was decked out in her White Sox jersey and matching scrunchie, which was gathering her gorgeous red hair in a high ponytail, and he, wearing his Cubs jersey and baseball cap, with his sexy face sporting his graying scruffy goatee, while their arms are wrapped around each other smiling as bright as the lights in Wrigley Field.

Exasperated, she thinks this ought to be a ton of fun explaining to her mother why she has allowed the wild daisies to over-run all of her treasured flower beds in the backyard, much less why she broke up with Danny, the son of her mother's best friend, and broke his heart.

Laying alone in bed in the same house she has slept in her entire life, she wanders back to this morning. Amy and Christine were so shaken and unglued regarding the hellish circumstances, but in her mind, nothing can be done except to be cautious and wait to see what plays out. She questions if she hadn't driven Danny out or had a husband or family of her own, would she too be more rattled and afraid? Danny was one of the good guys, and surprised by a rare tear rolling down her cheek, she questions, what the hell is wrong with her and why is she so damn afraid to commit.

By noon the next day, the Floridians have arrived, but for her folks, there is no Winnebago being towed behind a ten-year-old Buick. Stepping out from the shiny silver Infinity Q60 convertible, two still youthful seniors with smiling sun-damaged faces briskly start unloading their heavy luggage, assorted duffel bags and a bushel basket of bruised oranges.

The beep from the stainless-steel Braun coffee machine notifies the coffee is ready. The family is now planted around the maple kitchen table while her sweets-addicted mom is oohing and ahhing the delicious blueberry cheese coffee cake fresh from Wolf's Bakery, which Beth serves on her grandmother's heirloom crystal serving platter and causes another round of oohing and ahhing from her mother.

Her dad has lived in Florida for fifteen years now, yet not even an hour back in Chicago, and he has plenty to bitch about, especially her honor the mayor. On the other hand, her mom is clumsily scrolling for photos of her grandchildren on her phone. Beth's eyes ache as she tries to keep up with glimpses of photographs whizzing by of her sister's two high-school-aged kids soccer, basketball, prom, graduation and vacation photos.

That night, with her past pinochle skills failing her, she is buried by her dad during a competitive hour of three-player pinochle, and by eleven o'clock, her travel-worn parents can no longer keep their eyes open and decide to call it a night. Feeling like a little girl again, Beth smiles, remembering and welcoming back that same safe, comforting feeling of her childhood when she is lovingly kissed good night on the cheek by both her parents.

****

Stopping short when entering her section of the police station, Beth is baffled to see new recruit Vicky Alvarado rifling through the papers and notes neatly stacked on her desk. Suddenly, lifting her head, Vicky's face burns bright red, spotting Beth's enraged eyes drilling into her from across the room. Fuming, yet never speaking a word, Beth calmly advances to her desk, then swiftly and angrily yanks out the heavy metal desk drawer and ferociously slams it back in, exploding loudly with the force of a short-range ballistic missile, causing Vicky to flinch and burst into tears.

Kneeling on the hard tile floor and gathering the scrambled papers, victims of the desk slamming and now spread across the floor, Vicky apologizes profusely, explaining between sobs that it isn't what it looks like. She insists Captain Washington had read her the riot act minutes earlier after not receiving the Daily Violent Crimes Report, and she was backtracking and searching all desks she had previously delivered mail to, hoping to find the missing report.

The cynical person she is, Beth does not acknowledge her apology or explanation but dismisses her simply by placing her fingers face down under her chin, quickly flicking them out and upward with indifference, flashing the universal gesture for "Get Lost", and Vicky timidly scampers away.

Beth is pissed having to deal with this nuisance, especially after having to fight her way through the scuttlebutt infiltrating the police station this morning and flowing steadily from the never-ending gossip mill of the men and women in blue. There is talk of scrubbing the recently posted list of test scores for the Police Sergeant's Exam, the same test Beth painstakingly studied for and took two months ago and successfully landed in the top ten percent.

Captain Washington, in his wisdom, was responsible for convincing her to take the exam, as she never had any desire to climb the highly politicized ladder. She was always satisfied and content, wanting only to stay independent and secure in her standing as a skillful lead detective. Besides, she didn't play nice with others and was unwilling to play the crazy political games.

However, he explained that if she achieved the sergeant's position, which included a substantial pay hike, it would also significantly increase her monthly pension payment when she retired. Not only did she study diligently for the test, but failing to tell the captain, she invested some of her hard-earned savings making a purchase off the discreet city menu.

A private city service menu, recognized only in the secretive City of Chicago underground, allows citizens or employees to move to the top of the list for any city service or favor needed but can come with a stiff price tag.

While clerks, managers, foremen, ward superintendents, aldermen and higher-ups will claim there is a fair and non-biased way of requesting and receiving city services and coveted promotions that are fairly attained and achieved from top down, in date order and by highest test results, they are telling the truth. However, they may not be accomplished until Illinois turns from a blue state to a red one.

Nevertheless, you jump to the top of the established list when you contact the right person for the right price. The menu has prices from a mere twenty bucks to get a heavy-duty recycle garbage can to fifty dollars for rat poison to wipe out the entire family of long-tailed rats ferociously gnawing and burrowing into your basement. Costs can go sky high for transferring from one city department to another, and the crown jewel of fees, landing on the promotion list.

To order off the menu, the more expensive the item, the more complex and secretive it is. An excellent place to begin is by putting out feelers to other city employees and sitting back to wait for a call. Anyone and everyone employed by the City of Chicago knows of someone who is heavy with clout.

It took all of four days for "Tony" to contact Beth about the sergeant's exam, requesting she meet him at the noisy and crowded Dave Matthews Band concert at Northerly Island to avoid any unnecessary eyes or ears. Beth knew within minutes of meeting up with him, observing how he ogled her, it was evident she would qualify for the arm candy discount, and grasping that, she played it to the hilt. Months later, after paying him his outrageous cash fee, she was pleased to see the results of her posted test scores.

Aware of the risk she took acquiring Tony's assistance, she is old enough to recall the infamous Chicago Silver Shovel Scandal, only because her dad had met with a "Tony" back in the day, landing her the job with the police department during that time. This was a major United States FBI investigation into the political corruption in Chicago and eighteen individuals were handed corruption convictions, six being Chicago aldermen.

Concerned and worried by the rumors flying about, Beth slips outside into the parking lot and calls Tony, abiding by his rule never to text. Knowing he will never answer his phone, she leaves a brief message requesting he call her, then slipping the phone back into the rear pocket of her jeans, she returns to her hectic day.

Taking a shortcut back to her office by entering the rear of the building and cutting through the lunch room, the hairs stand up on the back of her neck when she spots Jessica Torres chowing down on a sandwich while her canine dog, Magnum, vigilantly poised and alert, surveys the room with his penetrating eyes. Disgusted, seeing who has joined her for lunch, her eyes bore into a chatty, happy-looking Vicky Alvarado.

Noticing her at the same instant, Torres smirks back at Beth just as vindictively, and as she takes a sip from the cup of coffee she is grasping in her hand, her middle finger shoots straight out, and she points it directly at Beth.

The blood drains from Vicky's frightened face as the other two confrontational women continue to hold eye contact, while a low menacing grr emerges from Magnum as Beth passes by and belligerently shouts out to Vicky, "Hey recruit, call animal control. They need to be notified there's a stray bitch loose in the lunch room!"

That afternoon, when Tony returns Beth's call, he arrogantly tells her she needs to let her gorgeous body chill, as there is nothing to be concerned about. However, if she is that worried, a little one-on-one time with him would assuredly seal the deal.

Enraged but not wanting to piss him off, she plays along, trading sexy innuendos and wisecracks, and agrees to meet him next Tuesday at the dark and dim Booze Box in Fulton Market for sushi and a Japanese Manhattan, hoping this time he remembers to wear deodorant.

Spotting the watch commander heading her way, she quickly disconnects the call with Tony. An old friend of her dad's, he smiles, inquiring about him and laughing, states that he hopes the old man is keeping a seat warm on his beloved Boston Whaler 345 fishing boat for his soon-to-be-retired CPD buddy.

Getting straight to the point, he reveals the station dispatcher has just received another call regarding a domestic disturbance involving Evelyn and Besart Vako, the young Albanian couple who call home a dilapidated roach-infested apartment above a cluttered hardware store on congested Division Street.

When originally called to the shabby apartment three weeks earlier, two beefy, muscular patrol cops had to wrestle the raging, hot-tempered husband to the ground while fighting to stop his brutal attack and continued walloping of his wife's already bruised and beaten body.

After the skillful officers had successfully yanked the husband's arms backward and tightly cuffed him, they patiently informed the couple that Besart would be immediately hauled off to jail.

Years ago, when cops would try to de-escalate a domestic disturbance, they would advise the husband to take a walk and cool down. However, they learned that once the officers left the property, the husband would return and beat the living shit out of his wife. The statute now is, if a spouse, either male or female, shows any sign of injury, the offending spouse is automatically taken to jail.

Hearing this news, his abused wife, seated in the corner of the shabby couch holding and consoling their shocked six-year-old daughter, immediately leaps up, tossing the little girl off her lap onto the floor and charges the officers.

Blaming not only herself but also the kind officers for being the source of her husband's violence, she slaps one officer powerfully across his face and reaching out with her other hand, grabs the other officer's hair, ripping it from his scalp. Screaming, she demands they not take her husband to jail, and if they do, they will be responsible for her plunging a knife into herself and her daughter, killing themselves before they even hit the bottom of the stairs.

Although detectives are rarely called in for domestic disturbances, this time, it was warranted that a detective complete an investigation into the unstable wife, considering the threats to harm herself and the child. It was Beth who met and conducted the interview with Evelyn.

Tears staining her plump ordinary face, Evelyn answered the door to the red-headed detective who was struggling to balance a box of Dunkin' Donuts along with a Walt Disney Frozen coloring book and crayons. The thoughtful gifts cracked the ice, and Evelyn stopped crying long enough to explain how stressful their lives had become since her hard-working husband had unfairly lost his job at Costco having been found intoxicated on the job.

She continued to detail why he should never have been taken to jail, leaving their family without him, and sobs she is the reason behind her husband's angry explosions. She tearfully explains, that it is her fault alone when he unwillingly hits her, made worse when he is drunk on vodka because he regrettably loses control and strikes her out of frustration. She pitifully confesses when he shouts she is too fat or she is too stupid to pay the bills on time or too lazy or doesn't cook as well as his mother, she understands if she could only change, so would he.

Although she has a grueling schedule of back-breaking tasks cleaning houses for a living and having to take public transportation to and from work, she is still expected to have a hot meal on the table every night for her husband. He blames her for the reason they do not have enough money to last the month.

She assured Beth she would never harm her daughter, who has just joined the ladies and is sitting between them on the couch, proudly displaying the beautifully colored picture she has finished. Acknowledging that sometimes her husband drinks too much, she insists she knows how to avoid his triggers after being married to him for six years.

Beth encouraged and supported her while providing the usual spiel on how important it is for her to overcome her damaged self-worth, and the steps she needed to take to allow her and her daughter to escape her husband's verbal and physical abuse.

Handing her a brochure for Naomi's Circle, a battered

woman shelter on Sheridan Road, and a card with her contact information, Beth stands up to leave. With her dark circled eyes glazed over, Evelyn promises her husband is sorry and this will never happen again. Hearing the door lock behind her, and numbed by this pathetic scenario repeated so many times before, Beth sadly predicts they will probably meet up again.

Evidently, the time to meet again is today, after receiving the harrowing call from dispatch that a boozed-up Besart was beating on his wife again. Deciding after tasting the Jani Me Fasule (white bean soup) his wife had simmering on the stove, he felt she added too much sweet paprika and using thick potholders to grab the handles, he tossed the entire pot of boiling soup at her full force, barely missing their young daughter.

Beth cringed and hated having to get involved in any domestic disturbance, never knowing how things would turn out, and usually not for the better. A 10-16 is one of the most common police calls received, and it is also the most dangerous call for law enforcement; it's the call every cop fears.

Entering the neglected apartment building, their noses immediately pick up the aroma of simmered onions, parsley and tomatoes. The young, fresh-faced patrolman accompanying Beth kicks aside the cigarette butts, broken glass and other crap strewn across the tiny black and white hexagon tiles in the vestibule and makes a path to the dark, steep stairs leading to the second floor, and both stare at each other questionably unaware of what is waiting for them inside the volatile apartment.

Reaching the top of the landing, they knock at the plywood door with the name Vako printed in distinct European script lettering. Inside, they can hear screaming from all three members of the Albanian family: father bellowing at the top of his lungs, mother screaming hysterically and daughter sobbing for daddy to please stop.

Getting no response to their relentless pounding on the flimsy door, the young patrol officer uses his powerful shoulder and easily breaks it down. Struggling to see while their eyes adjust to the poorly-lit apartment, it is evident the stained, threadbare shades have been pulled completely down and the lighting fixtures smashed. The rundown apartment is even more ominous, shrouded in darkness and shadows, as the afternoon sun trickles through the ripped shades, casting an evil disturbing glow.

Neither of them is prepared for what they are about to encounter. Both husband and wife are standing ten feet apart, pointing guns at each other, while their young daughter is standing evenly between them, crying and clutching a dirty, ripped Winnie the Pooh bear.

The patrol officer shrugs his shoulders and shakes his head in Beth's direction, acknowledging this is way above his pay grade. Neither of them has an opportunity to call for backup without taking the chance of their having their heads blown off, so Beth speaks first.

"Whoa," is the first word out of her mouth as she catches the attention of both Evelyn and Besart. He stops swinging his gun wildly and screams that the bitch has ruined his dinner, and she, looking like she is only being held together by a thread, shrieks she is going to kill him while the poor confused little one's head spins back and forth listening to each of her parent's deadly threats.

Making a split-second decision to negotiate with the crazed couple, she decides the husband is more of the threat and calmly addresses him, pleading he put down the weapon and discuss the situation. He yells back that he will only do so if his wife puts her gun down first, and she furiously shakes her head no, clearly having lost it.

Beth tries to imagine how unflappable Captain Olivia Benson of television's *Special Victims Unit* would approach the crisis. Not being Olivia, however, she struggles with how to defuse the volatile situation. Hoping their mutual love for their daughter may be the key, she asks the little girl if she wants Mami and Babi to make up and quit fighting.

Clinging to the grubby Pooh Bear, she acknowledges yes by

shaking her head briskly up and down as she swipes her greasy brown hair away from her dirty little face. Noting both parents' eyes tear up, she hopes this will motivate them to agree to lay down their weapons. If only the little girl had stood still, instead, she made a slow turn and started to walk to her mother, leaving the distraught husband to believe she had chosen sides.

Horrified, Beth sees his gun is steadily aimed not at his wife but at his daughter, feeling betrayed by the little girl. His cold, deadly eyes don't blink when he brutally pulls the trigger, shooting the six-year-old on the side of her head and setting off a terrifying chain reaction.

His horror-stricken wife, who has despised and feared guns all her life, clutches her gun with two trembling hands and shoots madly in his direction with three of the five bullets missing him, but two rupturing and tearing his chest apart, as he squeals like a wild animal and crashes to the ground.

Having one bullet left, she crams the barrel of the gun deep into her mouth, then shockingly and unexpectedly spins around, removing the weapon, and with an unhinged look on her face, takes deadly aim at Beth, ready to fire the final shot. Instantly, the loud blast from a gun rings out, but it's the crazed Evelyn who flies off the shoddy linoleum floor and is thrown into the cracked wall after being shot through the heart by the shaken patrol officer, who has now gained control of his revolver.

Beth rushes to the child, tugging the Pooh Bear from her locked arms, and forces it down on the side of her head, fighting to stop the gushing flow of blood, knowing the patrol officer throwing up on the kitchen floor has already called for an ambulance and backup.

Talking to the unresponsive child, she gazes at her parents' bloody, lifeless bodies, praying to hear the sound of CFD ambulance #15. With the first responders heavy boots hammering up the stairs and rushing into the apartment, the little girl, barely breathing, is hooked up to an IV, strapped onto the medical transport device and dashed out of the building while Evelyn and Bensart now lie covered in blue plastic tarps.

In Olivia Benson's world, the little girl's eyes would flutter open, and she would be adopted by two loving parents residing in wealthy downtown Manhattan and live happily ever after. And by the time the credits begin to roll at the end of the episode, the child actor will have already been cleaned up and munching on a burger. But, this poor kid will have the blood and stench on her for hours, and if by some miracle she does survive, after becoming a ward of the state and placed in a line of horrific foster homes, she will no doubt be starring in her own personal remake ten years from now.

As bad as this day has been, Beth's only desire is to go home and be greeted by hot, steaming water jetting down her aching body for a solid thirty minutes and to immediately pop an Ambien and hit the sack. Instead, she is greeted by her mother frying pork chops, but the delicious smell of the pork chops can't hide the foul smell of disdain and disappointment coming from her mother discovering her break-up with Danny.

****

With her folks leaving tomorrow, Beth is happy for the chance to spend a little one-on-one time with her dad. The day being so perfect with sunny skies and temps in the low 80s, they decide to walk the picturesque Tam Golf Course rather than take a golf cart and are only delayed once when a pair of Canadian geese decide to rest at the fifth hole.

Finishing up nine holes of golf, both Beth and her dad are famished, and as they wait to be seated at the Howard Street Inn, hoots and hollers erupt from the chaotic table of the same good old boys, who always wave to Beth and Moira, after recognizing her dad. Jumping to their feet and shoving back their chairs, they rush to their old friend and drag over two more chairs to their table. Surprised, to say the least, when they discover Beth also carries the silver shield, she is automatically accepted as their newest brother-in-arms.

Their boisterous laughter can be heard across the restaurant as they take turns running through their shenanigans of thirty years ago. The volume of the conversation only lowers and grows serious, and all heads turn towards her when someone questions if she's heard anything about the major corruption investigation about to drop.

Half the guys here, including her dad, acknowledge their kids were on the tampered lists for obtaining jobs with the city during the last investigation but fortunately weren't touched by the Feds because they were too low on the totem pole with the government only wanting to fry the really big fish. One retired First Deputy whispers he's heard this investigation is like Silver Shovel on steroids, and hearing this, Beth chokes back a mouthful of melted cheese and guacamole.

SEPTEMBER

Well, well darling mother, you do lead an interesting life. Not as interesting as mine, I'm sure. Looks like you've done pretty damn well for yourself after dumping me, so let me share a little bit of my amazing childhood all because of you selfishly doing just that.

A caring, elderly couple from a small town in Iowa adopted me, who were deemed too old to go through traditional adoption channels, but the devout Sisters thought they were good people. They weren't; they only went this route because they had arrest records in three states.

Kindly Ma loved to bake in her roach-infested kitchen and used her grubby Mixmaster to whip and beat ingredients for all kinds of putrid goodies to sell at seedy flea markets. Pa, however, enjoyed using his hands to beat and whip me and did so every day he was boozed up, which was practically seven days a week.

Both were fascinated with child beauty pageants, and they entered me for the first time when I was just a baby. I won third place, the first and only time I ever won anything, but according to them, I was on my way to the big time.

Plenty of used sequined and sparkly toddler-sized dresses and second-hand kiddie high heels could be found at Davenport garage sales, and Ma was good with her hands, be it sewing and altering dresses or slamming me across the face.

Just a toddler, Ma would layer and smear makeup on my baby face making me look like a little whore, which was exactly what she always called me, her dirty little whore. Years later, when I started growing up, now fighting to keep me childlike, it was Kmart frilly anklets, patent leather shoes and pigtails with large hair bows for me.

Ma and Pa said lots of talent scouts were interested in me, and I learned to recognize them and smile. They were the old geezers seated in the back of the audience with their eyes rolled upward and always tightly grabbing their crotches.

Growing up questioning Ma and Pa why they hurt me, they would angrily erupt and holler, "Because of your shitty birth mother! She's wicked and forces us to hurt you!" When I would question why I had to take my clothes off for the men taking my pictures, it was always a similar response, "Blame your bitchy birth mother, it's her fault because she ordered them to do it". Then when the bad men started hurting my wee, I no longer needed to ask because I knew who to blame, it was because you demanded they do it.

My folks loved the internet, not just the web, but the dark web, where all of those talent scouts would pay good money to take photos of me, and for a few bucks more, Pa would let them feel and squeeze whatever they liked.

I ran away to California when I was fifteen- years- old, or should I say, I screwed my way to California. By this time, I knew all the tricks of the trade and how to hook up with horny truckers at any local interstate.

Porn made me an incredible amount of money. Rather, hardcore porn made me an incredible amount of money, and I saved every penny and invested it in an online social media networking service called Facebook. Not only did the investment pay well, where I made lots and lots of money, but I also had lots and lots of new friend requests, requiring my services, which also paid me lots and lots of money.

Hence, I thought it was high time I spend my birthday with you this year, Mother, and celebrate by ripping out your stone-cold evil heart.

AMY

The smell of sizzling bacon drifts under the bedroom door, nudging Amy awake following the most horrible night of her life. Still dressed in her pajamas and dizzy from the prescribed medications, she staggers into the kitchen and watches Andrew standing in front of the stainless steel stove busily trying to wipe the grease splattered across the otherwise spotless cooktop.

Dropping the dish towel, he steps towards her, tenderly asking how she feels, and confesses he hopes she likes scrambled eggs because those are the only kind he can make.

The burnt bacon and cold eggs can't mask last night's image of the deranged monk and his high-pitched cackle while attacking her. Remembering her promise to Anna to check if the coffee pot was unplugged, she begs Andrew to run upstairs to do so, never wanting to climb those stairs again.

Hearing his footsteps descending the stairs, he returns saying, "All's good," but warns her the upstairs porch is a mess with smashed flower pots and potting soil spilled across the floor. Regrettably, he tells her the small Japanese maple tree that was tossed on its side, seems to be split in two, and there is a mountain of glass from whoever broke the ceiling and security lights.

Apologizing that he has to leave so soon, he explains that he must return to the office to assist his sister in preparing documentation for a high-profile motion that must be filed.

Instructing her not to worry, he advises he will have his admin contact a cleaning service to arrange for everything to be placed back in order by the end of the day.

Scanning her phone, she comes across a message from a Detective Fontanetta requesting she return his call. Upon doing so, he relays that CPD has received information regarding the clothing she described the monk wearing. It appears to be a costume that was discovered by a Streets & Sanitation worker, stuffed in a garbage bin near Amundson High School and has been forwarded to the Special Investigation Unit to examine. He suggests she be extremely vigilant and take extra precautions locking her doors and windows, and although short of manpower, patrol cars will be monitoring the area around her building whenever possible. If having a patrol car circle the block whenever possible was supposed to make her feel safer, it certainly didn't.

With Andrew gone, it isn't until one o'clock that she wrestles herself into the shower after receiving a call from Jaskowiac Janitorial Services, advising a clean-up crew would be out within the hour. Answering the door, she is surprised to see three sturdy sixty-ish-year-old women loaded down with brooms, buckets and cleaning supplies standing on the front porch conversing in Polish. She is even more surprised, exactly two hours later, when the porch is spotless with even the yellow and purple pansies having been replanted and the broken tree bound together with strips of torn cloth.

Having closely followed the emergency room doctor's instructions, she has iced her swollen lip religiously since yesterday. Removing the fresh ice pack just minutes ago and viewing herself in the mirror, she giggles, recognizing perfect Angelina Jolie pouty lips, and realizes by her laughter, it's the first step to getting back on track to her old optimistic self.

She even surprises herself by saying yes when Andrew calls later that afternoon asking if she is up to going out for dinner. Not needing to ask, he knows they will be cautiously descending dim steps down to the basement. Not her basement, however, but that of the Half Shell Restaurant on Diversey Avenue with the hopes Rocky has a table available in the even darker restaurant where no reservations are ever taken.

Rocky, the feisty seventy-year-old Italian waiter, having an unbelievable way of recognizing customers, greets them with his unmistakable Chicago accent, "How ya doin Miss King Crab Legs and Mr. Jumbo Shrimp?" and they follow him through the crowded basement to a table in the rear.

It's amazing how crab legs dipped in melted garlic butter, coupled with a glass of crisp white Chardonnay, shared with someone you love, can lift your spirits, and Amy feels just that. With Andrew spending the night again, the porch back in order and the police patrolling the area, she feels her life is returning to normal.

Driving the short trip home, she flinches, hearing her cell phone ring and recognizing CPD on the display. Apprehensive about receiving a call at this late hour from the Chicago Police Department, she nervously looks at Andrew and picks up. "My apologies, Amy," blurts Detective Fontanetta, "I know it's 10:30 PM, but I wanted to confirm all is good with you." Suspicious hearing the tone of his voice, she questions if something is wrong.

Hesitating, he discloses that a patrol car cruising by her building called in something suspicious to dispatch. Seeing the blissful look on her face abruptly vanish, now appearing frightened and alarmed, Andrew grows concerned and starts shooting off questions, making it impossible for her to hear and understand what the detective is saying. Informing the detective they are just minutes away, he notifies her that he is currently out front of her building and will be waiting for them to arrive and explain the situation.

Arriving in front of her house, there is no need for further explanation. Lights are blazing through every window in the building and are casting off a macabre presence as if evil itself is glaring down at her with hellish yellow eyes. Other houses on the block, hiding behind maple trees and veiled in darkness, appear frightened and cower in fear of the morbid building.

Struggling to catch her breath, she is terrified and grows weak in her knees, questioning how every light in the entire two-flat has been mysteriously switched on. Her eyes travel to every odd-sized window, not only from her apartment but the one above and the dingy basement, as she fixates on the lights erupting and cloaking the entire building in sinister brilliance.

Cowering, her eyes immediately dart away from the dirt-streaked cellar windows, seeing how the ghastly illumination has transfigured the gloomy basement into a jungle of twisted shadows where hairy inch-long centipedes and fat black sewer bugs are scooting across the damp floor, searching for cracks to hide.

Natural light reflects hope and safety and protection and security. But this light is just the opposite. She is terrorized by it. It is cold and threatening and brutal and barbaric, and she can see even the police officers clasping the handles of their guns are on edge and sense foreboding.

The two patrol officers enter the house first, and after a quick inspection of the first floor, Amy and Andrew are allowed to enter. Nothing appears to be out of place, but Amy can't shake the disturbing feeling of being watched and violated.

Both insist on tagging along behind the officers while they go about their creepy chore of traveling from room to room and closet to closet to switch off the intimidating lights. With the decision made to start from the top down, they march upstairs in single file and step into the Heiser's cozy apartment.

The serious officers stay alert and on guard, as they slowly and painstakingly inspect each room, praying some crazed maniac does not burst out to viciously cut their lives short, never having the chance to see their young children again.

After each room is inspected and given a thumbs up, Andrew follows through by switching off the lights, but Amy can't shake the image of talon-like fingers sneaking from room to room, flexing and treacherously flipping them back on.

Exhausted from the daunting task of inspecting every room,

and haunted by the ghostly glow and terrifying shadows cast on the walls, Amy grows more anxious with each passing light being switched off. Never experiencing this kind of terror before, when Andrew reaches out and turns off the final light in the basement, she is unable to breathe. Closing her eyes tightly and covering her ears, she fights but fails to keep the terrifying flashback at bay, and once again, the thunderous cackle from the grotesque monk blares through her ears.

With the police search finally completed, Amy hurriedly tosses her silk pajamas and a few necessary toiletries into her pink Victoria's Secret overnight bag, and she and Andrew depart for his 22nd-floor Lincoln Park condo, deciding it's safer to spend the night there.

Andrew, every bit as tense and tired as she is, swings his head sharply in both directions, checking traffic before pulling out and making a U-turn on Addison Street, and she remains silent, too frightened to share that she sees a lamp ominously glowing from the sinister second-floor apartment.

****

After two days, Amy is bored and growing irritable while staying alone in Andrew's fabulous condo, having nothing to do but wander from room to room, viewing the spectacular panorama of the lakefront. You can only watch so many sailboats sprinkled on beautiful Lake Michigan and crowded footpaths spilling over with joggers and dog walkers before you go crazy. She yearns for her toothbrush to be back where it belongs, sticking up from the pink plastic tumbler in her own modest bathroom.

Seeking to make herself useful after washing the breakfast dishes and spending time watching and laughing out loud at the hilarious WGN news anchors, she decides to tackle the monumental pain-in-the-ass job of changing the linens on Andrew's handsome black leather sleigh bed.

Yanking the bedding off is easy. The real challenge is stretching the lavish 700-count fitted sheet over his enormous bed without stubbing her pretty polished toe into one of the huge storage drawers situated under the bed, which he never quite manages to close. Just as she is deciding how to position the gray silk pillows on top of the luxurious matching duvet her phone pings with a text from Andrew.

Anxious to not only get back to her own place but hoping to return to the theater soon, she is ecstatic when he texts that he has rearranged his schedule for today and will drive her home this afternoon. Her nimble fingers immediately fly across the screen as she quickly responds with a thumbs-up emoji followed by three red hearts.

With her yellow straw purse draped over her shoulder and Victoria's Secret travel bag clutched at her side, she is more than ready to leave when she hears the chime from the private elevator, knowing nothing will stop her from instantly hopping in and jabbing the down button for the lobby. However, her mouth drops open, and she has to take that back after seeing a smiling Andrew stroll through the elevator door, balancing a hot, mouthwatering Lou Malnati's Pizza.

Opening the sliding glass patio doors, never worrying about locking them this high off the ground, he steps onto the magnificent balcony and places the steaming pizza on the table adjacent to the trendy black wicker patio set.

Before Amy gets the opportunity to drag him into the kitchen, requiring his assistance setting up the patio table, she for plates and silverware, and he for wine glasses and a bottle of cabernet sauvignon, he reaches for his weapon of choice. With fury in his eyes, he races to the far end of the balcony and ferociously bangs his war-torn broom on the balcony railing, hoping to be victorious over his constant battle between him and the loud annoying female pigeon cooing for a mate.

The sight of this meticulous, contained man losing it over a silly pigeon sets off peals of laughter from Amy, and when he joins in, they both collapse onto the cushiony wicker sofa, unable to stop giggling.

Appreciating the delicious butter-crust pizza and red wine while basking under the warm sun, they are jolted from the peacefulness of the lazy summer afternoon by the shrill sound of Andrew's cell phone.

Recognizing the number displayed from the incoming call, he wipes his sticky hands on the napkin and picks up immediately while Amy nervously watches his face turn somber and white. Visually upset and distressed, he continues to shake his head back and forth repeating the words, "I can't believe it, I just can't believe it."

Overhearing the one-sided conversation, she can only imagine something dreadful has happened to one of his parents. Hanging up, he tensely blurts out he needs to leave immediately for Northwestern Hospital, not for one of his parents, but for his sister who has just been rushed there by city ambulance after suffering a heart attack in the office. Worried and alarmed, he agonizes, knowing he must first call his mother to notify her because his father is so unnerved and shaken.

When his mother picks up, he catches giddy laughter and clinking glasses and realizes today must be her bridge day. Hearing her excuse herself from her friends and the noise surrounding her, he struggles to make the troubled call as palatable as possible. Not desiring to upset her any more than necessary, aware she will be in a panic driving back from Highland Park to the downtown hospital, he embellishes the facts and explains to her that Ashley has only had a mild heart attack. He stresses she need not worry but should take her time and be cautious when driving to the hospital.

Already corking the bottle and placing it in the side compartment of the fridge, Amy hustles him to the elevator, telling him to drive carefully and join his father as soon as possible. Tucking the cardboard tabs back into the top of the pizza box, she knows Andrew will welcome a piece when he arrives home hungry much later tonight, and after washing the wine glasses and dried-on pizza dishes, she scans the contact list on her phone and calls for an Uber.

Settling in back at home, she reviews Anna's instructions for the care of her plant babies and sees the African violets are in need of watering today. At first thought, she is hesitant to enter the second-floor apartment but decides to nevertheless and climbs the stairs and enters the silent, stuffy apartment. Checking each plant individually, she knows Anna will be pleased with how well they are thriving, and after completing this task, she now looks forward to going back downstairs to enjoy a long soak in a relaxing bubble bath in her own jacuzzi.

With hot water filled nearly to the top and covered with fragrant rose and lavender bubbles, she closes her eyes and relaxes while hearing the sound of the gate next door clanking shut from the open bathroom window.

Hearing the excited voices of Kareem and Elijah, the little kids who live next door, she listens to their sweet conversation after rescuing an injured beautiful yellow swallowtail butterfly, a prized catch seldom found in the city. Kareem is complaining that his younger brother has punched the holes way too small in the shoe box for the butterfly to breathe, as Elijah is pulling out grass by the handfuls to cover the bottom of the box and throwing in a pink petunia for the butterfly to eat.

She has to keep from laughing out loud when their mom calls them in for dinner, and they discuss where they can hide the box so their dad won't find it, remembering she did something similar when she was a young girl. One more impatient shout from Mom, "Dinner. Now boys! And don't forget to shut the gate." Knowing this time Mom means business, she listens to their shuffling feet, hurrying through the gangway and the banging of the metal gate.

Tomorrow she plans to be back behind her desk in the bustling theater office, concerned she is already past the deadline for totaling the final count of special guests and invitees for the Salvation Army's yearly fundraiser and benefit, which includes a special performance of *The Sound of Music*. She needs to sit down with Donna and painstakingly go over both the A list and B list of names for the seating plan, and she crosses her fingers that the multi-skilled production assistant has already started preparing it.

She reminds herself that the names of the newly elected mayor of Lincolnshire and town officials need to be verified for correct spellings and proper titles. Also, there is always the additional worry that compassionate Captain Swenson of the Salvation Army, who is notorious for responding late with his list and always up to his neck in the latest catastrophe, will have invited an additional twenty guests at the last minute.

After confirming and tallying the number of guests, she will subtract that amount from the 850 seating capacity of the theater and distribute the remaining seats to underprivileged children in the Chicagoland area. The same children gifted with these tickets and receiving the rare exciting chance to experience a live theater production need to be prepared to stand and strain their little necks to view the stage, as the dignitaries, dressed to the tens, will take up the best seats in the house.

Soaking much longer than she had expected, and the gangway now perfectly silent, she looks up towards the window surprised to see how dark it is outside, and reaches for her towel. It feels good to dry her hair with her own familiar towel, and she drops it to the floor, swishing it around with her foot to soak up the water that has splashed from the jacuzzi.

Wiping the condensation from the mirror, she adjusts the framed picture next to it, showcasing a panoramic view of the stunning Colorado Rocky Mountains behind the inscription of her favorite quote, "Life Can Change in an Instant" and fondly remembers having purchased it years ago at an art fair in Galena.

In this case, life can change not in an instant but in the time you take a hot, relaxing bubble bath. Opening the bathroom door, she is confused as to what her eyes are drawn to. Paranoid, since last year experiencing a problem with water leaking into the upstairs apartment, which constantly dripped in through the crown molding and took the roofer three attempts before locating the actual leak, she now immediately freaks out at the first sight of any suspicious drop of water. This is not a drop nor a puddle but a small river traveling down her hall floor.

Bending down to get a better view of the trail of liquid, she runs her fingers through the watery, white fluid streaming down the hardwood floor and realizes by the sweet slightly sour smell that it is milk.

She now knows and understands that unless an individual has been personally affected by a stalker, it is impossible to feel the sheer terror of knowing that someone is secretly watching you and patiently waiting for any chance to confront you when you are isolated or alone. The stalker may not even hate you, and in his twisted mind, he may actually believe he loves you.

A car parked in the alley honks in the dead of night, the telephone's shrill ring at 6 o'clock in the morning, a phlegmy cough under a window slightly ajar on a hot summer evening, a sudden thump from the empty apartment above – normal sounds for anyone else, but for Amy, they now automatically trigger terror, and her heart stops cold as she prays it isn't him.

Being all by herself, such as now, is when her imagination really kicks in and nothing can slow the beat of her frantic heart. She is terrified, realizing someone has slipped into her apartment while she was soaking naked in a bathtub behind an unlocked bathroom door. He is close enough to harm her, yet he chooses instead to quietly steal into her kitchen and slowly pour a gallon of milk across the kitchen floor, trailing down the hallway, just to greet her when she opens the bathroom door.

She cannot imagine what kind of psycho would take the foolish chance to break into her home with the pure intent of scaring her. Why her? Does she know him? Does he take some sort of warped pleasure, knowing the constant fear is more excruciating than an actual attack?

Part of her wishes this monster would just get it over with instead of prolonging the agony and keeping her locked in the nightmare that is now her life. She asks herself if this is the effort of a madman or if could it be a brilliant individual attempting to gaslight her. Nevertheless, he or she must be pleased, as they have succeeded in turning her into a neurotic woman who is no longer capable of doing even the simplest of tasks without looking over her shoulder in fear.

Reaching for her cell, she wonders what a 911 operator would presume of her emergency call, reporting a gallon of Dean's 2% milk escaping from her fridge and cruelly being sucked up into her newly refinished hardwood floor. It would definitely be a call shared and hilariously laughed at by co-workers seated around the bar, sipping on bottles of cold Miller Lite after a long day of answering life-threatening emergency calls. Realizing she can't possibly bother Andrew with this lunacy, she calls and leaves a voicemail for the detective.

Wringing out the sopping towel into the bathtub while milk runs down her arms, she struggles to grab the jangling phone. Detective Fontanetta admits he is dumbfounded regarding the bizarre events befalling her but regrettably concedes there is nothing further he can do other than send a tech out to take photos. Although deeply concerned, he offers his opinion that most of these strange mishaps have been designed to scare her. Mishaps she thinks angrily, has he already forgotten the rock slammed over my head in the cemetery and how my lip was split open?

Although sympathizing with her, he woefully advises that last year the city of Chicago experienced almost 26,000 violent crimes and 797 murders, while nineteen of the twenty-two police districts saw an increase in sexual assault reports, with reports nearly doubling in an area including River North and parts of downtown.

She acknowledges to him that she realizes her fears and anxieties are at the very bottom of the totem pole of concerns for the Chicago Police Department. What is so terrifying to her is, if she knows it, and the police know it, so does the sadistic madman.

The detective does have one suggestion, however, which is to have an alarm installed. Having crossed her mind years earlier, she quickly abandoned the idea, fearing her elderly tenants would have too much difficulty operating a complex alarm system. Thanking the detective, she informs him she is one step ahead of him, and a service tech from ADT has already been scheduled to consult with her tomorrow regarding the installation of their premium system.

Wanting to stay awake, hoping to hear any news from Andrew, she is afraid to take any Excedrin PM, which could knock her out for the night. Once he does call, it is after ten o'clock, and he conveys that he and his parents are still at the hospital, waiting for word regarding his sister's condition as she is still undergoing surgery. Sounding exhausted, he discloses the doctors have advised the family to expect a long night and begs her to try and get some sleep, promising her he will get back to her first thing tomorrow morning.

****

Andrew's sister Ashley, heavily medicated and out of recovery, is resting in a private room after last night's successful open heart surgery. Dr. Rabinowitz and her thankful family met in her 16th-floor room earlier when her eyes slowly fluttered open, and she immediately swore off smoking for the rest of her life.

Entering the crowded hospital cafeteria, Amy spots Andrew's mother waving her hand in the air. Maneuvering through the heavy lunchtime crowd of hospital employees, she grabs a napkin to brush off the crumbs on the plastic chair and joins Andrew and his thankful, relieved parents.

The food is better than expected, and they celebrate Ashley's successful surgery by dining on cold turkey sandwiches along with mustard potato salad piled on limp lettuce. Disappearing for a brief time, Andrew returns, handing her a packet of mustard for her sandwich.

Gaping at him as if he is crazy, she reminds him she doesn't like mustard, and it's obvious the packet has been sliced open. He grins, insisting he is sure she will adore this particular variety of mustard, and now it's his parents who have joined, staring at him as if he has lost his mind. "Just open the damn thing," he playfully banters. Withdrawing the smudged packet from his hand, she rips off the remaining top, and three sets of eyes pop wide open when a breathtaking two-karat solitaire diamond engagement ring smothered in mustard falls out.

Clapping erupts as doctors, nurses, hospital visitors and cafeteria employees stand up and applaud, while his smiling father and teary-eyed mother join them, observing Andrew down on one knee and Amy crying and wildly shaking her head yes.

****

"Where should I place the candy bags for the kids?" yells out Miguel, the maintenance man who has been graciously helping set up the theater for tonight's benefit. Amy points him in the direction of the gaily-draped table, surrounded by a massive display of bright, colorful balloons featuring every color of the rainbow, which is sitting outside the entrance to the auditorium.

By three o'clock, the noise and enthusiasm level has been taken up a notch as musicians, talented performers, exceptional lighting men, temperamental chefs and wait staff sporting comfortable shoes start to arrive and do their best to avoid bumping into each other while rushing to their designated work areas.

There is always apprehension and uncertainty at the start of every performance, be it the remote possibility the sound system malfunctions or the violinist's car has broken down again, but the one thing she has no anxiety or concern about tonight is the actual play. Poppy has been flawless, and even Donna has stopped complaining about her.

She is excited to have the chance to wear the gorgeous black and white shimmer gown she wore previously when accepting the Midwest Guild Director's Award. This time, however, she has the perfect shoes. Reaching into the tiny closet in the corner of her office, she pulls out the hanger, rips away the clear plastic cover protecting the gown, and carefully steps into it, knowing the guests will start arriving shortly.

Listening to the sweet strains of *Edelweiss*, performed by the delightful string quartet, she gazes at the fashionably attired women and men attending the black-tie affair who are chatting and slicing into juicy cuts of prime rib prepared to perfection by Chef Franz and his staff.

Seated at the table next to the dignitaries, besides herself, Andrew and his parents, are Captain Swenson, the Executive Director of the Salvation Army and his wife, and the President of Highland Park Hospital and her husband, and it is easy to spot Andrew's mother vigorously bending the ear of the hospital president throughout dinner.

With the chocolate-swirled cheesecake being served and the speeches about to begin, she sees a troubled-looking Donna hurriedly crossing the room and approaching her table. She bends over and whispers into Amy's ear that the yellow school buses are pulling into the driveway earlier than expected, but that is not the problem.

The problem is Poppy has still not arrived. Amy's fingers fly across her phone, frantically sending a text questioning her whereabouts, and five minutes later her heart sinks when she receives a reply.

Poppy's text begs forgiveness, regretfully explaining she was invited to a last-minute audition for a WTTW promo, and it ran longer than expected. She is still stuck at the Morton Arboretum in Lisle. Fortunately for her, she is still in the running, but unfortunately for us, there is no way she can possibly return by the opening curtain; this followed by a series of three sad yellow faces with tears dripping down.

Ordinarily, this would never be a problem, but her understudy had called in sick earlier with a raging sore throat and a 103-degree temperature. The blood drains from Amy's face, and she immediately excuses herself from the table, hurrying out of the banquet room just as the new mayor steps to the podium.

Being the worst possible time for this to happen, she has only one recourse. She can step in and play the role of Maria. She did so beautifully twenty years ago and can certainly fake her way through the dialogue, knowing most of it by heart.

However, the big question is, although she still has

a perfectly well-toned body and is undoubtedly still very attractive, can she pull off being a forty-six-year-old Maria, matched with a twenty-eight-year-old Captain von Trapp, who is young enough to be her son?

Having no time to think, the answer can only be yes. Immediately explaining the bizarre turn of events to Andrew and the mayor, she races off to hair and make-up to start the process of being transformed into the youthful Maria. Carefully removing the diamond hair ornament from her glamorous updo hairstyle and swiftly brushing it out, her ebony hair is meticulously styled into wholesome milkmaid braids.

With a still vibrant voice and the poise and agility of a twenty-something-year-old dancer, she easily falls back into the role, perfecting the sweet, mischievous essence of Maria and finds herself loving it. Goosebumps rise on her arms, hearing the thunderous applause of the audience amidst the scene of the von Trapp family singing at the music festival, awaiting their planned escape from Austria.

The audience sits in silence, staring at the moonlit stage, observing the backdrop of the beautiful Switzerland Alps. The child actors, who are wrapped in scarves and winter hats, walk up the stairs behind a prop depicting the mountain, which the audience visualizes them climbing the frigid Alps.

Eyeing the final child beginning to descend the stairs, it is Amy's cue to climb to the top for her final solo. The orchestra launches into its intro while the spotlight follows her precisely as she begins ascending the stairs. Abruptly and unexpectedly, a powerful explosion thunders high above the stage, and the gigantic overhead spotlight bursts and shatters, triggering dangerous sparks and glass to rain down on the stage like a giant roman candle, and the entire auditorium is thrown into total darkness.

With the chaos and pandemonium of fire alarms blaring, the kids crying out for their mommies and the adults pushing and screaming to be first heading out the exit doors, Amy feels a tug at her ankle, and losing her balance, falls from the top of the prop and crashes to the floor.

CHRISTINE

"Ready now Christine. Relax and raise your head slightly. You will only feel the slightest pressure from the scissors," says the husky-voiced Dr. Marinov. It has been one week since the prominent plastic surgeon stitched her slashed face. Returning to the University of Chicago Medicine River East to have the stitches removed, she only needs to look at the surgeon's pleased face to know he has been successful.

With his hand scribbling a prescription for scar cream and 100 SPF sunscreen, he speaks in his thick Russian accent and suggests she stay out of the hot sun for the remainder of summer. However, understanding that will be next to impossible, with her having four small children, he stresses the importance of not forgetting to wear sunblock daily.

Reporting there is no sign of infection, he admits to her she is indeed a very lucky woman not to need corticosteroid injections because the lesion is healing nicely on its own. He further explains if she does not experience any further swelling or itching, she should make an appointment four weeks from now.

She is taken aback when he switches gears and questions if the police have any leads or suspects regarding her attack. Regretfully, she tells him no, explaining the police have informed her the probability of solving the crime is next to impossible. Besides there being over four hundred prominent guests, wait staff and caterers to be interviewed; the police have learned the security guard who was stationed at the front entrance admitted to leaving his post unattended to sneak in his girlfriend and take her on a tour of the glitzy gala, which allowed anyone from the public to freely enter the building.

She has no reason to explain anything further to him. However, she does and continues to tell him exactly what she has disclosed to the police. Presuming she was alone in the restroom, she was terrified when someone charged out from behind a stall and angrily grabbed her from behind. This deranged individual fiercely yanked her hair, whipping and painfully pulling her head backward. Being in a state of shock, the only thing she clearly remembers is the swift, searing pain from the razor-sharp blade slicing into her skin and did not realize she was injured until she saw her horrible bloody reflection in the mirror. Unfortunately, the only detail she could provide the police was hearing the swishing rustle of a woman's ball gown exiting the bathroom.

After the automatic gate lifts and Charles pulls onto Grand Avenue, exiting the hospital's underground parking lot, he poses the question she has been dreading. He asks, realizing they are not that far from her mother's assisted living facility, if she would like to pay a visit. The silence is deafening as she vigorously shakes her head no.

Following the attack, Charles requested Dana Rae cancel all of his appointments and meetings and has been a solid rock for her and the children, even promising them a sleepover in the yard tomorrow.

When the car door swings open and before Charles and Christine barely exit the car, their little noses remarkably smell the crispy, mouth-watering Popeye's fried chicken, and the hungry boys come running and swarm around their parents. Markie is the only one who looks sad, and when Christine questions him why, he answers sadly because she hates him.

Christine looks devastated and pulling Charles aside, voices her serious concerns about the child, posing the question if it might be time to consider seeking professional counseling for him. However, the last thing he ever wishes to hear is the thought of any of his sons being flawed in any way. He insists the boy only craves attention, especially with her confined in the hospital last week and having to fend for himself while his other brothers teased him. She wants to scream, having learned long ago that Charles has one customary smug reply when addressing any of her concerns regarding any of their sons. "Stop your needless worrying, they'll outgrow it."

The next day, the kids remain on their very best behavior, aware that the day of the long-anticipated King Family Camp Out has finally arrived. However, no blankets and card tables for the great outdoor Camp Counselor Charles King, instead, he made a special trip to Dick's Sporting Goods and purchased a North Face Wawona six-person tent sight unseen.

Born in Chicago, and living in the treacherous Cabrini-Green public housing project, he has never camped out his entire life. In his neighborhood, there was no rule for kids to come in when the street lights came on because there were no street lights that ever came on. All were destroyed or broken, with shattered pieces of glass littering every street corner from bullets shot by gun-wielding gangbangers who plagued the treacherous streets day and night.

Growing up, he would frantically dart up the cracked concrete stairs, two steps at a time, racing to his cramped 14th-floor CHA apartment only to find his strict no-nonsense mama holding the belt waiting at the top. He discovered early on that you didn't mess with this woman's rules, especially the one having to be in their apartment by sunset. Learning the hard way, his cries could be heard from behind closed tenement doors, and he never forgot the one and only whupping he ever received from his loving, God-fearing mama.

It seemed like the unfolding would never end as Charles opened and spread out the huge one-page sheet of instructions needed to assemble the giant six-man tent. Taking one look at the step-by-step directions, he made a desperate call to Tammy and paid her current boyfriend a bundle of money to assemble it.

The sun finally starting to disappear has the excited boys running back and forth, filling the enormous tent with their favorite toys, snacks, drinks and sleeping bags. The tent is set back far enough from the main house, sitting in the middle of a cluster of enormous oak trees, to have the feel of being deep in the Wisconsin woods, yet close enough to run back for the forgotten bag of Oreo cookies.

Almost wanting to join them, witnessing how much fun they are having, Christine remembers this is a boys-only trip. Besides, Charles has warned her about the need to keep her face clean and free from infection. With hugs for each of them, she leaves the tent, and while turning, shakes her finger at her husband, reminding him of his promise of no ghost stories.

With the woodsy aroma of the night air breezing through the open bedroom windows, and her family camped out under the stars, she grows nostalgic, imagining the same charm of a 1950s kind of summer as she listens to her noisy, laughing children starting to quiet down and fall asleep one by one. With the chirping crickets and the lulling sound of the cicadas, she too, drifts peacefully off to sleep.

Waking in the middle of the night, not from a nightmare but a wondrous dream about the family on vacation, splashing in the warm, aqua waters of the Caribbean Sea, she remembers she has forgotten to apply the scar cream to her face before going to bed.

Needing to get up and use the bathroom, she decides it is better late than never to apply the cream. Mindful she has kept the tube in the same corner of the vanity having to apply it so often, she is confused when it's nowhere in sight. Trying to recall if the boys have been in her bathroom, she is positive they have not.

Sliding the mirror to the left of the wide LED medicine cabinet, she discovers the ointment propped up next to her vitamins on the top shelf, and a note, written in a small child's scrawl, flutters to the ground. Retrieving and examining it, she instantly rips it up, flushing it down the toilet after gawking at the awful words "Die Mother".

****

Hearing the clatter of dishes rattling in the kitchen and the fighting over the last strawberry pop tart, she knows the campers have survived the night. Everyone but Charles. She has never seen him look so exhausted. With his sunken, sleep-deprived eyes and the gray whiskers sprouting from his unshaven face, he looks as if he has aged ten years and curses the salesman at Dick's who promised he would never regret purchasing the king-sized air mattress for a restful night's sleep.

"Don't slam the door," yells Charles, and with the loud bang of the door slamming, the boys run outside to play. Sitting together at the breakfast bar, both working on their second cups of coffee, he breaks the unexpected news he is flying back to DC this afternoon.

He reveals that Dana Rae phoned last night, advising him of the urgent need to return to the office, having been absent for the last few weeks. Standing up from the kitchen stool and hugging her, he explains he has everything under control and that he will be back by the weekend.

He confesses he has already contacted Tammy and discussed an agreement with her to become the family's live-in nanny with the plan for her to temporarily move into the larger of the two lavish guestrooms. He assures her this is a win-win situation as Tammy will oversee the boys full-time while she gets back on her feet, and he can return to key foundation endeavors without needless guilt about abandoning her and the family. Pouring his now cold coffee into the sink, he hurries past her, calling over his shoulder that he needs to quickly pack and shower if he wants to make his flight on time.

As the limo is disappearing down the gravel road, it passes Tammy's older model Ford Focus heading to the house, and the two cars kick up stones at each other. Stopping, with both vehicles rolling down their windows, Charles and Tammy stare at each other, and Charles purrs, "Be sure to take care of my girl!"

The boys flock around Tammy and eagerly insist on helping carry her belongings up to her new room while she cheerfully grabs little John and places him on her hip, so he too can tag along. Bouncing on the bed with the boys, her eyes check out the plush room that will be her home for the next few months, and she wonders how she will be able to sneak her boyfriend in.

Shouting out one of their favorite questions, Tammy cries, "Who wants to go swimming?" and Matthew, Mark and Luke scatter to their rooms to grab their bathing suits while she searches to find John's suit. Without enough time or energy today for her to pack up the kids and cart them to Silver Lake, they march the one hundred feet to their own inground swimming pool, nestled between the shady oak and weeping willow trees.

The ten-foot sandbox adjacent to the pool is huge. It has more than enough sand for the rambunctious boys to build forts that hold off marauding Indians while strategically placing the little plastic Civil War soldiers, cowboys, horses and Indians. However, not wanting to play in the sand today, the older kids grab their noodles and dive into the pool. With each of them being excellent swimmers, she keeps one eye on the kids, and grabbing a bucket and shovel, sits down with John and using her finger, writes the name of her dream man in the sand.

Not returning until just before dinner, Christine waits at the front porch with the water hose while Tammy lines up the hungry boys, needing to be hosed down from the sand, before heading into the kitchen for supper.

Only seven o'clock, but with last night's camping trip and spending the day outside swimming under the hot summer sun, the children have grown tired and ornery. Christine offers to help Tammy with their showers and get them ready for bed, knowing exactly how tiring and difficult this final chore of the day can be, and they decide to divide the kids. Christine takes Matthew and Mark as they are old enough to shower by themselves and only need to be supervised and toweled off, plus, she won't have the extra worry of getting her scar wet bathing the younger two boys in the bathtub.

She places the toilet seat down to sit and supervise Matthew, who is arguing he absolutely does not need a shower because he has been in the pool all afternoon. Finished toweling him off and only needing help when he struggles to pull his T-Rex pajama top over his wet head, it is Markie's turn.

Markie is her only son who favors her with his fair complexion and fine blonde hair, so opposite his other brothers, who all have their father's coffee-colored skin and dark tight-curled hair.

Searching for him, she finds him in his bedroom, already having fallen asleep in his bed and cringes, aware he will not only be crabby when she wakes him but will then refuse to go to sleep feeling wide awake. She calls his name softly and gently shakes him to wake him up.

Sand spills across the Italian marble tile floor as she tosses his now dry bathing suit down the built-in laundry chute and coaxes him into the shower with a bribe of peanut butter cookies and a glass of milk after he is finished and in his pajamas. Not until after adjusting the water temperature and scooting him under the spray does she notice the deep blue bruises covering his little round butt.

****

Don't ever believe little boys forget; they don't. Rushing down the stairs for breakfast today, the first thing out of their mouths is when will they be leaving for Great America. This is the day of the rescheduled trip after the original was canceled due to that torrential rainstorm.

Christine explains that Tammy has already left to pick up her mother, who will also be going to the amusement park. It is well worth the extra cost she is paying the two women, especially Tammy's responsible mother, Viv, who she knows will keep a close watch on little John and take him on the kiddy rides while Tammy whoops and whistles with the older kids on their favorite roller coasters and gets drenched on the water rides. Hearing the muffler on Tammy's car backfire, she knows the two women have arrived. No longer a guest, now a family member, Tammy does not knock, but she and her mother step through the porch door and enter the kitchen.

Checking off her list of items for the park, Christine hands Tammy the emergency kit, bags of snacks for the kids, cash and her credit card. Meeting her mother previously, Christine is confident she is up to the job of watching active two-year-old John, who is instantly taken with her, and shrieks with joy when she hands him colorful pipe cleaners that he instantly is infatuated with bending and twisting them while blessedly, not a bang, pop, or whistle can be heard.

Not trusting Tammy's noisy Ford Focus, she hands her the keys to the Cadillac Escalade, and they all pile in like a traveling circus. Ambling back to the house, she stops to adjust the cushion on the relaxing porch swing, deciding to take a moment for herself. She sits down, and her feet gently glide the swing back and forth before she heads into the house to pick up the trail of clutter left behind after preparing for the big trip.

Even though Immaculate Home Cleaning Service does a deep cleaning of the house once a week, there is always a task that needs to be attended to in a house this size. She is certainly not opposed to hard work but the clean-up seems to be endless. Grabbing the broom, she sweeps under the kitchen table, cleaning up the crumbs from this morning's breakfast, and tosses them into the tall stainless steel garbage container, which definitely needs emptying soon.

Continuing upstairs, she makes her daily round of emptying the wastebaskets in each of the bathrooms. The white plastic bag is nearly filled to the top with tons of crumbled Kleenex, brown-tipped Q-tips, makeup-covered cotton balls, an empty box of Mr. Bubbles and two crunched-up toothpaste tubes. Hoping she has enough room in the Hefty bag, not needing to run downstairs for another one, she smashes the trash down, providing room for whatever rubbish is left in the fourth and final bathroom. Immediately entering the room, she spots the water in the toilet smack to the top of the rim, slightly trickling over and forming puddles on the spectacular tile floor.

Damn, she thinks, Markie has struck again, and God only knows what he has flushed down the toilet this time. Having the plumber on speed dial, she telephones her and is thankful when Cookie picks up. Nervously laughing, she advises her it is the client who keeps her business thriving and once again desperately needs her aid. Taking a minute to assess her busy schedule, Cookie informs her she has a job in her neck of the woods later this afternoon, and can stop by afterward, but can't promise what time that will be. Christine sighs in relief and assures her it is no problem as she will be home the entire day.

Although her fingernails and toenails are screaming manicure, all previous thoughts of having a mani-pedi this afternoon have vanished, knowing she needs to be available for the plumber. Gathering an emery board and OPI Infinite Shine white nail polish from her bathroom, she plans to do her own nails after lugging the stuffed garbage bag downstairs and into the kitchen.

Only hoping to make one long trip to the garbage bins outside, she reaches into the stainless steel kitchen container to also grab that bag. Pushing down on the garbage already inside, to draw the strings together and secure it, she touches something round and solid. Having no idea as to what it could possibly be, she cautiously searches the bottom of the bag and retrieves Markie's treasured autographed Cubs baseball.

After returning the baseball to her son's bedroom, she finds it ironic that finally being alone on a peaceful day and having loads of time and energy to work in her beloved flower garden, she is held prisoner on the gorgeous wrap-around porch, hiding from the sun rays under the cool shade. So wishing to tend the lily-of-thevalleys that desperately need to be thinned out, she sadly recognizes it is more important she stays out of the sun, not wanting to harm the healing scar.

On a beautiful day like this, it is a sin to be sitting inside, but that is precisely what she is doing as she flicks through the 102 stations on Direct TV, not finding anything to her liking.

Hearing a car pull up, she drops the bag of pretzels and rushes to the door to see Cookie hauling her heavy toolbox up the porch stairs while trying to stop the sweat from rolling down her weary face.

The tired-looking plumber climbs the stairs, following her down the long hall into the bathroom with the clogged toilet. After inspecting it, she informs Christine that she has her fingers crossed that the problem is nothing like the intensive project from the last time.

Carefully using the electric drain auger, it only takes minutes for her to yank out a Peppa Pig Weeble. Christine instantly feels guilty, already having blamed Markie, as this may well have been the handiwork of her two-year-old, following in his older brother's footsteps because pink Peppa is one of baby John's favorite toys.

Finishing the job quickly and effortlessly, Christine thanks Cookie and asks her if she would like something cold to drink. Hurrying to pick up her tools, she tells her no thank you, explaining she needs to return home to her kids, having promised that she and her husband would take them swimming at the community pool in town tonight. She goes on to say that she is so lucky and grateful to be married to her husband, Ryan, who is a wonderful father to the girls. Even after spending nine hours on the top of a hot, scorching building today, laying heavy asphalt shingles and doing the back-breaking work of a roofer, he would never dream of disappointing his girls.

With that, the floodgates break, and Christine bursts out crying. Embarrassed, she reaches for a Kleenex and blowing her nose, apologizes to Cookie, explaining she has been so stressed lately with the slew of strange and mysterious episodes occurring in her life, and Markie being just one of them.

Cookie admits she has a soft spot for the little boy, as he often keeps her company when she works on retrieving his frequently submerged toys. Hearing this, she sobs even more so and pours out her heart regarding her concerns for her son.

She whimpers that he has always been her shy, quiet son.

The good boy. The boy who is most sensitive and kindhearted, who would always share a toy and politely say thank you without being prompted by Charles or herself. She confides that his behaviors have become increasingly bizarre with angry outbursts and the paranoid belief that someone is trying to kill him. Weeping, she agonizes that his bad behavior is escalating and discloses the details of the horrible note she discovered in her bathroom medicine cabinet, fearing it came from him. Admitting she needs to seek professional help for her son, she confesses she is frustrated with Charles blindly denying the problem and refusing to support her, which has led to her feeling overwhelmed and abandoned. Cookie finishes wiping her greasy hands on the soiled rag, and not having a clue how to console the distraught mother, tries to sympathize but can only whisper a heartfelt, "I'm so sorry."

****

"Quit throwing rocks, you're going to hit someone in the eye," Christine yells at Matthew from across the driveway. The three older boys are growing impatient, waiting for their father's limo to arrive. With Tammy upstairs getting ready to leave for the weekend, she has been singing to her youngest and gently gliding on the porch swing.

Hearing the sound of crunching stones, they take off flying down the road before she can shout for them to be careful. Minutes later, she laughs out loud, eyeing Sammy, the limo driver, slowly navigating up the driveway and waving his hat at her from the window. The shiny black auto pulls up with the trunk wide open, and the giddy boys crouched in the trunk squashed between Charles' luggage. I'm sure Charles thinks the welcoming committee is for him alone, but it's just as much for Sammy and the coveted trunk ride.

Plucking the kids out from the trunk one by one, the first words out of their mouths are, "Can we Dad? Please, can we go Dad?" Christine holds little John's hand as his amber eyes grow wide, and he screeches with joy, recognizing his father. He waddles towards him while his chubby feet rotate in the rocky gravel, and when Charles swoops him up over his head, the child giggles wildly. She is amazed how Charles can sit for hours in a crowded sold-out flight and still look chic and sophisticated, never even loosening his tie.

As the gang traipses into the house, Tammy is just leaving and seems to be surprised to see Charles. Offering a nervous rushed hello, she sails down to her car, having scheduled this weekend off to spend time with her mother, or so she says.

Allegedly only eleven still exist in the state of Illinois, and they are lucky enough to be a short drive away from one of them - the McHenry Outdoor Theater. Both Charles and Christine know the boys' questions earlier of "Can we Dad?" meant only one thing. They were asking, well more like begging, to go to the McHenry Drive-In tonight to see *The Incredibles*, one of their favorite Disney movies. He has been promising all summer to take the kids, and they never let him forget it. From the sounds of the cheering and clapping, Christine knows tonight he has relented.

Removing the hot pepperoni pizza from the oven, she serves the pieces on flimsy paper plates while Charles is upstairs showering. Popping a strand of mozzarella into her mouth, she smiles, announcing to the kids what the next task will be after they have all finished eating. More cheers ring out, and this time for her, with everyone wanting to pitch in and help make the popcorn and afterward each getting to pick out one snack to take to the movie.

After loading the car and arriving at the outdoor theater, Christine, staring up into the night sky, notices how dark it has grown and observes the man in the moon is nowhere to be found. The mosquitos are thrashing against the car windows, fighting to get in, and the one caught inside is furiously buzzing around Christine's ear as she struggles to swipe at it with her free hand.

Her youngest has already fallen asleep in her arms, and it appears Charles may not be far behind. Still, the boys in the back seat are wide awake and excited as they jump up and down, cheering on Mr. Incredible, his wife Elastigirl, and their three amazing kids, Violet, Dash and Jack-Jack.

Driving back home and surveying the damage, Christine knows the thirty dollars she will spend tomorrow at the Roadway Car Wash for the super deluxe car wash will be well worth it. Plus the additional ten-dollar charge for extra vacuuming should do the trick, ridding the car of any leftover popcorn from the outrageous popcorn fight the boys had on the way to the drive-in.

Navigating slowly and following the perfectly spaced solar lights down their long dark driveway, they are both startled when they arrive at their home, which is now ominously hidden in the black of night. Alarmed to see neither has remembered to turn the porch lights on, or leave a light burning in the house, the menacing silhouette of the towering residence unnerves them. More disturbing to Christine, is gazing into the distance and seeing the ghostly glow of the swimming pool lit up from the luminous underwater pool lights, knowing they have not been turned on for days.

Charles, not liking this for a minute, picks up little John, who is still clinging to his bunny, while Christine wakes up the other boys, who have fallen asleep on the ride home. They tumble, one by one, out of the car, and Charles guardedly leads them through the chilling silence to the front porch, guided only by the haunting sound of the wind chimes.

Christine is through the door first, and after entering the security code, she hurriedly starts turning lights on in the house while the children, too tired to climb the stairs to their bedrooms, plop down on the comfy floor cushions in the great room.

Incredibly, the porch and house now ablaze with light, have chased away all earlier fears, and she shouts to Charles that she will head down to switch off the pool lights, realizing if she doesn't do it now, she will be too tired after getting the kids to bed.

Insisting he will do it, baby John, still in his arms, wakes up and starts fussing. Studying Charles now, he does not look like the dapper man who briskly stepped out of the limo earlier today. He looks beat and jet-lagged with his chinos wrinkled and milk stains from John's sippy cup covering his shirt.

Exasperated, she moans, "Honestly, Charles, it is much easier if I shoot down to the pool and turn the lights off rather than explaining to you where the light switch is located. By the time you get John settled into his crib, I will be back in the house, and besides, there is absolutely no need to worry with you back home with us." Charles, still hesitant, suggests that before he carries their son upstairs, he will wait on the porch until he sees she has turned the pool lights off.

She agrees, and quickly hikes through the dew-covered grass under the starless sky towards the pool. Seeing the moths fluttering about, she cringes, thinking of the bugs that invade the pool at night. Turning her head, not wanting to glance into the pool, she avoids seeing the skimmer bugs, with mouthparts too blunt to bite humans, furiously skirting across the water while the predator backswimmers, with their long oar-like hind legs, lurk upside-down, eager to inflict their painful bite.

Eventually, witnessing the pool lights turn off, Charles breathes easier. Unexpectedly, a gut-wrenching scream echoes out, replicating the cry of an animal brutally snared between the razor-sharp teeth of an animal trap, and he knows it's Christine. Just as quickly, the pool lights flash on again, and nearly losing his balance, he hustles as fast as he can while carrying the extra weight of his son to discover Christine's limp body floating in the pool with the horrid backswimmer bugs racing towards her.

BETH

"Hey Dorner, can O'Malley and I bum a ride to the green line?" Beth shouts across the room. "Ándale," he shouts back over his shoulder, and Beth and Moira grab their purses, chasing after him.

Both having to appear in court today at the Richard J. Daley Center, they agree it is best to take public transportation. They plan to meet up later this evening to throw back a few in celebration of Buddy Frank's early retirement. Beth is definitely looking forward to flaunting her bank shot while shooting pool and breaking the balls of fellow macho officers at the Aberdeen Tap in West Town, knowing it will assuredly be an Uber kind of night.

Choose any color-coded rail line in CTA's rapid transit train service: pink, orange, yellow, purple, red, blue or green, and any cop will tell you, that the red line is by far the deadliest. However, the green line, the only one to be heard rumbling while staying elevated above street level from start to finish, is a close second, where any random resident or visitor can go from citizen to deadly crime statistic in a minute. Armed robbery, assault with a deadly weapon, rape, murder - take your pick the green line has it all, so it's not surprising, climbing up the stairs to the platform, both detectives' eyes are focused and alert, searching in every direction.

The platform is already packed this early in the morning, and the two detectives discuss the court cases in which they will be appearing as witnesses and providing testimony during bench trials today. Beth's case involves a twelve-year-old kid, who carjacked a Chicago police sergeant's BMW from the Jewel parking lot one morning before school. Moira is testifying against a band of gypsies, who while living next door to Chicago Engine Company 68, took every opportunity to loot it whenever the firefighters got called out on a run, going as far as stealing a pork roast, cooking in the oven.

"Hey Moira, what did your mam use to say about bad pennies?" asks Beth. Moira's feisty County Cork grandmother had a proverb or old saying for just about everything, and the phrase Beth was trying to think of was "A bad penny always turns up", which came to mind instantly when she spots Torres and her dog Magnum quickly descending the stairs and exiting the transit station.

Go figure; just as the gruesome twosome leaves, while glancing down the long tracks searching for the headlight from a far-off train, she spots what seems to be a small group of frightened bystanders. They are depositing their phones and wallets into a duffle bag held by a scrawny teenage girl while another grossly overweight blue-haired one is waving a Glock semi-automatic pistol in the air. More troubling is she is sure Torres had noticed this same group of victims before leaving Dodge.

Drawing their guns and coolly strolling toward the teenage robbers, they get close enough to shout "police". The high-as-a-kite skinny girl nervously spins around and clumsily dropping the bag high tails it down the stairs. The other one, now crying and panic-stricken, points the shaky gun in the officers' direction but decides at the last minute to toss it onto the tracks. As she swings around, her huge, thick thighs rub together as she waddles as fast as she can trying to escape. The detectives don't even give chase, knowing the gang-banger boyfriend parked below has probably already whisked them away in his two-bit get-away car.

With loud rap music blaring from the hooptie, the junkie

driver is no doubt already blowing through stop signs, speeding towards his seedy slum apartment, eager to deliver the brutal beating they will receive for failing to secure enough cash to pay for their next pathetic fix.

Some individuals in the crowd, perched on the graffiti-covered platform have failed to lift their eyes from their cell phones, viewing this as just another everyday big city occurrence. In contrast, others meander down the tracks to scope out what transpired and observe Beth painstakingly divvying out the contents of the loot bag to their rightful owners. At last, the train slowly creeps into the station, but with one look at the chaotic commotion, the worried train conductor accelerates and abruptly swishes past the outraged crowd.

Departing the courthouse, they admit the day has been a total bust. The twelve-year-old kid appeared in court wearing a Boy Scout uniform, looking like the all-American boy, and the crazy gypsies overran the courtroom, wailing and placing curses on the judge. Glad it's behind them, Moira steps onto Washington Street and flags down a cab, instructing him to drop them off at their favorite cop bar, the Aberdeen Tap.

Strolling into the booming crowded bar, the other cops start banging their beer bottles on the tables chanting "Ooh La La, Ooh La La". "God, you would think after all these years, these idiots would find something better to do with their beer bottles," complains Moira.

Beth laughs and yells over the blaring music, "Hey Pedroza, the spread's minus 150 for the Sox to kick your Cubbies asses tomorrow. Best you jump on it." "Yeah, I'll jump on it all right, the same way you wish you could jump on that stud firefighter I saw you pictured with in the Trib last week. You know, the one showcasing the annual Police vs. Fire charity game at Grant Park," he roars.

Pulling out the vacant stool next to Captain Washington, Beth sits down while raising two fingers, signaling the bartender for two bottles of Corona. Passing one to Moira, who hustles down to join her EMS pals in the back of the bar, she catches up with the Captain.

"You next Cap? You getting tired of babysitting us yet?" she asks, thinking that the sixty-three-year-old is looking every bit of his age lately. "Might be sooner than you think," he regrettably says, downing his third Makers Mark. "But what the hell, we're here to celebrate Buddy Boy's retirement. Where is the old bastard?" he snorts. And with that, he seems to have returned to his old self.

Another Corona," asks the cute twenty-something bartender, and Beth shakes her head no, saying she's already reached her limit for the night, and going forward, it's just ice water with a nice slice of lemon. Eyeing the world-weary Captain, she asks, "Upstairs or downstairs?" and removing his rugged hand from the bottle of beer, he slowly points his bent finger downwards.

Carefully making her way through a dusty storeroom and descending rickety basement stairs, she follows the smoke from Marlboro cigarettes and Cohiba cigars, hearing the muffled racket of shuffling cards and chips being tossed and anted into the pot.

Exploring the damp basement, there are just as many cutthroat women as men playing poker at the three large round tables. It's a game that takes an hour to learn but a lifetime to master, and Beth has mastered it pretty damn well, competing since she was a six-year-old with her dad, her grandpa and her teddy bear.

There is only one well-enforced rule for the five-hundred-dollar buy-in game: a player is required to remain in the game for a minimum of one hour before cashing out. No win one big pot and boogie on home. Texas Hold Em is played most often, but it is always dealer's choice, and wild cards are forbidden. Her personal choice is the hefty-priced Buy-A-Card with the high diamond in the hole splitting the pot. Every poker player has a favorite game, and this is hers, the one that never fails to bring her back.

Routinely stacking her chips, and aware when she is ahead,

she cashes out from the game three hours later, and without her chair getting time to cool off, another hungry contender slides right in. Tucking away her fourteen hundred dollar winnings, soon to be placed directly in the hands of the HVAC repairman, she calls it a night and waits outside for the Uber driver to pick her up and whisk her back home.

****

Welcoming the day off, and appreciative for last night's poker game, which not only kept her clear-headed but hangover-free, she is up early to enjoy a run through the Dan Ryan Woods before the thermometer hits the wicked ninety-degree mark that the WGN weatherman has promised for today.

Also, and always up early, are her elderly neighbors, Flora and Billy Higgins. The frail old man has already yanked the cord on his deafening lawn mower, causing the sleeping neighbors to groan and turn over in their beds, while Flora, decked out in her floppy sun hat, is busy digging out dandelions and shouts out a bright good morning to Beth.

Picking up the buzzing first, then glancing at her newly mown grass, it's difficult for Beth not to miss the ridiculously large pile of dog shit being attacked by swarming flies. Storming back into her house and returning with a plastic Jewel bag clutched in her hand, she disgustedly scoops it up, and Flora vigorously shakes her head no when she asks if she knows who the culprit is, knowing not much gets past those old, observant eyes.

Unlatching the side gate and taking long, angry strides to the alley to chuck the foul-smelling bag into the garbage bin, she is gifted with another gross mound, sitting in the middle of her expensive cobblestone patio. There is absolutely no doubt in her furious mind, considering her large backyard is fenced in, that this can only be the handiwork of that bitch Torres via her canine Magnum.

Sharply turning into the county forest preserve, she recognizes that blue-blinking lights are never good. So, instead of parking in her usual spot, Beth drives towards the flashing squad car parked on an odd angle under the cluster of high-branching Hickory trees near the running trail. More concerning and worrisome, is the fact that a crime has been committed in her own neighborhood on the same path she runs religiously three times a week.

Revealing her shield to the tall, slender patrol officer, who is off to the side talking into his walkie-talkie with dispatch, he tips his head to acknowledge her. He lets her approach the squad car, where a young woman is crouched in the corner of the back seat, violently sobbing while clutching the heavy cotton blanket wrapped tightly around her.

Identifying herself as police detective Elizabeth Crowley, she slides in, and squeezing next to the victim, she compassionately asks her name. "Angie. Angela Ritter," whispers the traumatized, young woman gasping for air as she tries to speak. Patiently questioning the distraught young woman, she is horrified to learn, amid spurts of sobbing and gagging, that she has been brutally assaulted after having been forcefully dragged into the heavily wooded area and viciously raped at gunpoint.

The alarmed patrol cop joins the women, and sticking his head into the back of the car, advises Beth that the day just got a hell of a lot worse. He relays that Region 11 Chicago Emergency Medical Services has just been activated due to a horrific chemical plant explosion on the far south side of Chicago, and according to the top brass, it is now all hands on deck. "Just go, I'll drive the vic to Little Company of Mary Medical Center," she barks, and minutes later, with the blue lights again flashing, the ear-piercing siren screaming, and the heavy smell of burnt rubber, he peels off towards congested Western Avenue.

Having gained her composure, Angela slowly opens up to Beth on the short ride to the hospital. She uneasily discloses, she is one of three siblings who grew up and were raised on their parent's dairy farm just north of Kenosha, Wisconsin. Furthermore, she attended the University of Madison, where she received her degree in agriculture, and had just accepted an incredible job offer at the Chicago High School for Agricultural

Sciences. The first time Angela seems to unknot is when Beth acknowledges she is very familiar with the four-year magnet high school, devoted to teaching agricultural science to urban students, as it is located in the Mt. Greenwood area of the city where she lives.

In a flash, however, she is sobbing again, expressing how uncomfortable it will be having to notify her worrisome parents regarding the rape, knowing they continuously fear for her safety living in a large city. She swears to Beth, having just relocated from her previous job in Milwaukee, that she recognizes the perils of the big city. Additionally, she always wears reflector athletic shoes, never runs at night and carries the Mighty Claw for protection.

The automatic doors swing open as they enter the hospital emergency room, and Beth displays her badge, identifying herself as a police officer. She and Angie are ushered into a cold private room where they are advised a nurse will be in shortly to explain the rape kit procedures, which causes more tears from Angie. Aware she is terrified, Beth volunteers to stay during the procedure, and she stops whimpering just long enough to whisper thank you.

Within ten minutes, a compassionate middle-aged RN enters the room, and after introducing herself, she questions Angie if she has showered, bathed, used the restroom, changed her clothes, combed her hair or cleaned the area where the attack occurred. Speaking for her, Beth explains to the nurse that the assault is very recent, just occurring within the last two hours, knowing it is critical any evidence needs to be collected within seventy-two hours of the incident.

The nurse briefly explains to Angie what a rape kit is and does. She advises it is simply a medical kit used to collect evidence from the body and clothing of someone who has been the victim of a rape or other kind of sexual assault. It contains a variety of swabs that are used on the genitalia, cervix, and the inside of the mouth to collect bodily fluids such as saliva and semen, which can help identify the perpetrator of the rape. It is also used to gather and store fibers from her clothing and hair, which eventually can be used to prosecute a rapist.

Keeping an eye on Angie, Beth catches her beginning to buckle when the nurse discloses after the initial collection of forensic evidence, a blood test is conducted to check for pregnancy or sexually transmitted diseases and infections.

Angie cracks when she simply tells her she will need to see her own doctor sometime within the next two weeks to review the test results because he will be the one responsible for prescribing treatment for any positive results. Hearing this, she drops to the tile floor and breaks down, not about the vicious rape or her defiled body, but the fact that only being in Chicago for two days, she has no doctor. Beth and the nurse struggle to get her back on her feet, both fully aware when a victim is traumatized as badly as Angie is, it can be the slightest and most unexpected incident that causes them to shatter.

Seated in the examining room outside of the thin plastic screen, Beth can hear the conversation between Angie and the RN. With her legs clamped in stirrups, the nurse winces, seeing her flesh torn open and bleeding from the gashes covering her inner thighs, and she sympathizes with her having to endure a violation this horrific. It is then Angela discloses that when the rapist discovered her Mighty Claw, a self-defense tool with sharp retractable claws designed to capture the DNA of an assailant, he was enraged and ripped it off her wrist and viciously turned it on her. With the nurse constantly reassuring her she has no reason to be ashamed or embarrassed, Angie also timidly confides the rapist wore a condom.

Driving her back to her apartment, Beth regrets pushing it, after repeatedly questioning if she can provide a more detailed description of her assailant. "I've tried Beth, I really have," she cries, "I'm so sorry. All I remember is he was short and a black ski mask covered his face. Wait! I remember he wore ridiculous red shoes. They were expensive, red Puma running shoes. Oh my God, how absurd is that? What kind of idiot am I to only remember shoes?"

Beth's heart drops while flashing back to the horrible nightmare of her own rape, never forgetting the gray and red Nike Cloud Trainers worn by the brutal gang member who viciously assaulted her thirty years ago and to this day still haunts her. Filled with compassion and taking an instant liking to the Wisconsinite, she graciously says, "Tell you what Angie, I'll stop at Tata's Pizza to grab you a beef sandwich, and then I'll check out your apartment to make sure you get safely inside for the night."

****

Three weeks later, recently retired Buddy Franks, who has now joined the retired cop club, sitting around the table at Tam Golf Course, makes a prediction stating, "I don't care if half the city hates her, this mayor has bigger aspirations - like governor, and that's why heads are going to roll regarding these payoffs."

Moira and Beth, who were outed by Beth's dad during his recent visit, have since become the mascots of the group, having been discovered they too, bleed cop blue and now always have a seat at the table. Beth dwells on how incredibly fast scuttlebutt travels through the police grapevine and also how much is proven to be fact. "So when do you think it will break?" she is quick to ask. "Any day now Ooh La La, any day," reports Buddy.

After finishing off the best taco salad and guacamole around, Moira lifts her golf clubs into the back of her Jeep and asks Beth if she wants to head east and catch the night game at the friendly confines. In her usual manner, Beth sticks her tongue out like she is about to puke and gives her the raspberries. Beth is a diehard White Sox fan, and the only Cub games she will ever plop down her hard-earned cash on are for the annual city series when the two rival teams duke it out, three games played at Wrigley and three at U.S. Cellular.

Driving down the expressway with all the car windows rolled down, Beth belts out the lyrics to *Bed of Roses*, chorusing along with Bon Jovi, and it reminds her when she gets home, she best go straight to the backyard and water the long-ignored, wilting red and white impatiens she has planted under the magnolia tree. Before the song has ended, however, she is interrupted by a call from Angie asking if she would like to meet up and go for a run later tonight when it cools down.

Beth is thankful Angie can't see her face, aware she is incapable of hiding her disdain. Yes, she thinks, she is a nice girl, but this is the exact reason a cop doesn't get too close to a victim. Angie has been using her as a crutch, having adopted Beth as her new best friend. Moira is Beth's best friend, and even she knows to keep her distance.

Her initial mistake was picking up the beef sandwich the night of Angie's rape. Beth felt sorry for her after being attacked, alone in a new city and possibly having an empty fridge. She had only planned on handing her the sandwich, and after inspecting her near-empty apartment intended to leave. Although nothing was out of place or even looked suspicious, Angie frantically threw herself on top of the duvet, crying and begging her to stay a bit, so Beth reluctantly did.

Following that, the reasons and excuses to be near Beth kept piling on. Such as, "I owe you for the yummy beef sandwich, my treat" or "I'm sure my apartment door has been tampered with, can you please stop by for a quick looksie", even, "I baked my mother's favorite recipe for chocolate chip cookies to thank you." Every time Beth tries to beg off, she plays a different pity card, and she is damn good at it.

"Haven't you started your new job at the agricultural school yet?" Beth irritably asks. "No. The principal has been so kind and gracious in advising me I should take as much time off as I need," she cheerfully replies. Again, Angie annoyingly presses her on how she is hoping they can meet up for a run later today. Beth curtly answers, "No. I have been golfing all morning, and I just want to take it easy this afternoon. Got to go," and abruptly disconnects the call.

Now home, pissed with herself for becoming so enmeshed with the ever-annoying Angie, she no longer has the desire or energy to drag the green plastic hose around the house and into the backyard to water the poor neglected flowers, much less hose down the patio.

Instead, she searches the fridge and pops off the lids of two giant Tupperware containers, one filled with strawberries, blueberries, and chopped pineapple and the other with fresh orange slices. Placing a large scoop of fresh fruit into the bottom of the largest glass she has, she fills it with chilled sangria and a long extra pour of VSOP brandy.

Adjusting her Apple ear pods, which are tuned to the White Sox game, she grabs the sweating glass and walks into the yard. She kicks off her sandals and plops down onto the yellow-flowered patio chaise just in time to hear the crowd roar, as first baseman José Abreu stretches out to make a phenomenal catch and ends the inning.

With too much golf under the scorching sun and way too much doctored sangria, Beth is startled to feel Mrs. Higgins from next door shaking her. Apologizing, she says, "Oh dear, I'm so sorry to frighten you, but I was out sprinkling the lawn, and your friend walked over, worried when you didn't answer your door, so I became concerned. I told her to wait out front while I checked the backyard, and thankfully you had just fallen asleep in the sun. She will be so relieved."

Beth recalls filling her glass two more times before passing out, and her head is thick and fuzzy. She walks with Flora to the front of the house only to see Angie standing there dressed in a skimpy summer dress, with a colossal grin slapped across her face, and holding a pizza. "Your favorite," she proudly gushes, "I thought I would surprise you with a large Al Capone special from the Wise Guys on 111th Street."

"How the hell do you even know where I live?" fumes Beth. "Don't you remember, you told me when I said I would be teaching in Mt. Greenwood," she nervously stammers. "I absolutely never gave you my address," Beth angrily snarls, instantly causing huge tears to start flowing from Angie's sad, shocked eyes.

Believing it to be far easier to invite the self-conscious woman into her house for pizza, and then explain why this has to end, rather than doing it in her front yard, where the nosey neighbors from across the street are already eyeing them, Beth half-heartedly apologizes and invites her in.

Already tense and feeling suffocated by this woman, Beth's only intention is to grab a bite of pizza and get her the hell out of the house so she can breathe again. Angie, blind to her bluntness, suggests it would be fun to eat outside on the patio, but Beth nixes the idea, grumbling it's not a good thought because the aggressive bees in Chicago go wild this time of year. Spotting one wildly buzzing on the kitchen window, she grabs a paper towel to smash it and discovers how it found its way inside her house – the kitchen window she permanently keeps locked and never opened is lifted just a hint.

"How's counseling going," Beth flatly asks, not interested in the least. "Really, really well and better than I expected," she excitedly replies. "I've been heeding the advice from the rape crisis advocate, and I now recognize I am a survivor and not a victim. I also want you to know I'm trying not to be a burden. It's just that everything is so overwhelming, and I'm having a really hard time trusting anyone".

Feeling this is the perfect opening to explain to Angie exactly why it is not healthy to maintain and build on this relationship with her, Beth runs down a laundry list of such reasons, from both her professional and personal points of view. Expecting tears and seeing none, she is surprised when Angie agrees and says she understands.

After the sun has set, and staying just long enough to toss out the paper plates and napkins, Angie joins Beth at the sink and stepping closer to her, whispers, "As crazy as you think I am, you'll probably think I'm even crazier, but I swear I just saw a woman with this huge dog in your yard."

Sandals smacking, Beth grabs a flashlight and bolts through the patio doors into the sticky summer night. As the sudden beam from the flashlight scares fat nightcrawlers back down their holes, the light slowly searches back and forth across long black shadows and lands on the back gate, which is standing wide open.

Bolting across the backyard to the open gate, she points the flashlight up and down the dark alley with not a soul in sight. Pivoting around, she turns and runs back to investigate the perimeter of her house. Methodically walking around it, and finding nothing out of the ordinary, her foot suddenly recoils, feeling her bare toes tangled and trapped in a wispy spider web. Swearing up a storm, after not discovering a thing, she has no choice but to angrily return inside the house.

Drenched in sweat, and already planning the countless ways she is going to torture Torres, she returns to the kitchen and finds Angie sitting at the table, lazily thumbing through what looks like old, time-worn photographs. Angie sheepishly asks if she would be interested in checking out her adorable baby pictures. "Not really," Beth rudely blurts out. "How about you just grab the leftover pizza and head on home."

"Hell no bitch!" Angie hisses. Violently flinging the snapshots at Beth's face, her thundering voice echoes across the room, "Hey Mother, just for old time's sake, why not take a peek at my fucking baby pictures!" Stunned and speechless, Beth flashes back to the unhinged woman who contacted Sister Eleanor months ago, seeking to locate and kill her birth mother. She can't believe Angie may be that same crazy woman who now imagines she is her mother.

"Listen, Angie," she says, but Angie stops her and shrieks wildly, "It's not Angie bitch, it's September." "Angie or September or whomever you may be, you are one hundred percent mistaken because I am definitely not your mother!" Beth yells emphatically. "Besides, what proof or evidence do you even have confirming this crazy belief?"

September details how she started the ball rolling after obtaining birth records confirming she was adopted from St. Philomena's Maternity Home in September 1992. After paying a private investor handsomely, he sifted through old public and church records, discovering the names of three girls from St. Philomena's who all gave birth to daughters in September 1992, but that was where the trail went cold.

However, diving deep into the murky waters of the dark web, it was easy after she contacted a mysterious, nameless individual. She provided him with the names of the three girls who could each possibly be her mother, and he identified that person as Elizabeth Crowley by the end of the second day.

Frustrated, Beth sighs, "Angie, the dark web is rife with con artists preying on suffering people all the time. They search for any opportunity to catfish anyone for even the smallest amount of money. You made it easy for him by providing three names, and all he did was go Eenie, Meenie, Minnie, Moe and his slimy, money-hungry finger landed on me."

Having none of this, September pitches the beer bottle across the room, shattering it into dozens of pieces, and Beth realizes the situation is escalating. She makes a sudden start to charge her but freezes just as quickly, now looking down the barrel of the SIG Sauer P238 pistol aimed straight at her. With Beth's Smith & Wesson secured in her bedroom safe, she has no recourse but to try and play out for time.

Patiently listening as September spills out the horrific details of her abused life, Beth tells her how genuinely sorry she is but respectfully repeats none of this is her fault. September rages that it is her fault and her fault alone after she heartlessly decided to wrap her in a big pink bow and gift her to those sick, old perverts.

September flings her head back and laughs maniacally, spouting that she, like thousands of other little bastards who cower in their beds at night, learned early on exactly what came next when daddy crawled under the covers.

But it was when daddy was drunk as a skunk, or on Sunday afternoons, when she would hear the television blasting from the front room and daddy yelping and cheering on Brett Favre's latest touchdown, that it was far worse. This was Mommy's turn, who could only be turned on by my pain.

With the string of twinkling lights shining on the patio, Beth blinks, catching a glimpse of Torres crouched down next to the Weber grill, gleefully watching the terrifying ordeal. Aware that Beth has spotted her, she slowly rises and mockingly points her gun directly at her.

"You know, I thought about throwing acid in your pitiful face, but this is easier," September spitefully laughs, still pointing the gun directly at Beth. She pleads with September to put the weapon down, telling her again she is making a huge mistake as it is impossible for her to be her mother. "Why should I believe your shit?" screams September. With seldom-seen tears streaming down her heartbroken face, Beth cries out in agony, "Because my daughter is dead! My baby was stillborn!"

SISTER ELEANOR

Slowly skipping down the narrow hall and squeezing Papa's hand, her frightened eyes flicker across the row of empty straw-filled cages at Lincoln Park Zoo. Growing closer to the last cage, her ten-year-old heart pounds with anticipation and fear, knowing who is caged there. His monstrous roar resonates and echoes across the zoo when he grows angry and mightily stretches his muscular 6'2" body upright while fiercely and powerfully beating his massive long-haired chest. Bushman, the most famous, terrifying gorilla in the world.

Prying open her tightly closed eyes, she sees him docilely seated on a wooden stump, staring out at her from behind piercing black eyes in an oversized head. With an unexpected thunderous roar, he leaps through the air, throwing himself against the steel bars of his cage. Terrified and swinging around to grab Papa, she turns her head to the side only to see the beautiful, young bride patiently standing in the long line of spectators waiting her turn to view the exhibit.

Jolted awake from the terrifying nightmare, Sister Eleanor's eyes lock on the rotating blades of the old, hypnotizing ceiling fan. Long-forgotten superstitions flood back, recognizing that seeing a bride in one's dream signifies death, and she begins praying for the three women.

With wrinkles sprawled across her sweet old face, hands bent by arthritis and watery eyes, she fondly recalls holding her Polish babcia's hand trudging down Noble Street on her way to morning Mass at St. Stanislaus Kosta School. Times like this were when Grandma Pawlina would share stories of her beloved homeland's old traditions and strange superstitions.

Little Eleanor knew if she told her she dreamt of seeing thick smoke or filthy water the night before, she would clutch her chest and warn her in broken English to be extra vigilant, as this was a troubling sign of very bad news. Whenever Grandma saw a bride in her dream, believing it meant death, Eleanor would hear Grandma's needle-point slippers shuffling to her old highboy dresser in search of her rosary beads.

Throwing her stocking feet off the bed, one leg at a time, and reaching for her glasses, she finds the dizziness has returned. She wonders if she needs to have her eyes examined, as she has been having difficulty seeing lately, and this morning the numbness in her right leg has only grown worse.

Trying to stand, she crashes to the floor, and as if God is watching over her, Marlena, who is stopping by her room to join her for morning prayers, discovers her. Hysterical and screaming for help, Marlena drops to the floor and lifts her white-haired head from the pool of her own vomit she is drowning in.

Reaching her as quickly as possible, it is still too lengthy of a drive for the McHenry County Paramedics to arrive before she suffers a life-threatening stroke, which leaves her unable to walk or speak. Sirens blaring, she is transported to the Northern Illinois Medical Center for treatment, and then days later, she is moved to St. Peter's Convent to recover, looking at years of challenging physical therapy to rehabilitate, if ever at all.

AMY

ComEd is quick to apologize for the power surge that caused the lights to blow in the theater. An angry father, who was turning around to smack his kids as he struggled to stop them from fighting, lost control of his Chevy Blazer, which plowed into a utility pole on Route 12, downing the wires and triggering the unfortunate mishap.

This satisfies the mayor, the electrical supervisor of the theater and Andrew, who logically explains to Amy there was nothing nefarious about her accident. He theorizes in all probability, she stepped on the hem of the long cape of her costume, which wrapped around her ankle and caused her to tumble from the platform. However, Amy vehemently disagrees.

After joining Andrew's parents, Brett and Claudine, in the limo, they drive back to the city, and Andrew spends the night with her, thankfully having no encore performances of blazing lights, freaky monks or trails of milk.

The next morning, they plan their day over sesame seed bagels and freshly squeezed papaya juice from Whole Foods. Andrew's sister, Ashley, is being released from Northwestern Hospital at noon, and he is chauffeuring her to their parent's opulent residence on east Cedar Street in the Gold Coast, where she will be recuperating for the next few weeks. Trying to imagine his mother playing the role of nurse, they both break out in giggles.

With a ton of laundry to keep her occupied, Amy mentions to Andrew she must remember to make a final trip upstairs to water the African Violets before the European travelers return from their trip next week. It will be a welcome relief hearing the Heiser's footsteps ambling above her again while the music of Nat King Cole, Perry Como and Andy Williams trickles down through the vents.

She makes a mental note to herself to stock their fridge so provisions are in the house the day they return. Staples like fresh-squeezed orange juice, a quart of whole milk and bottled Ice Mountain water, plus deli-sliced Krakus ham, Jarlsberg Swiss cheese and soft onion rolls for sandwiches should do nicely. Then, possibly a drive to Lutz Bakery on Montrose Avenue for a flaky cherry strudel if she has time.

The lonely echo of the door closing after Andrew's kiss goodbye, triggers disturbing thoughts just as Mother Nature turns hostile and heavy clouds roll in from the storm brewing over Lake Michigan. Praying the aged catalpa tree in the small patch of front lawn doesn't topple over, she stares out the window as it buckles from the huge gusts of wind and struggles to stay upright. She wonders if Andrew has arrived safely at the hospital or if his wiper blades are frantically clashing with the deluge while battling to keep the windshield clear.

Hair flying straight back, she fights the gusting wind as she climbs the stairs to the second-floor porch. Along with the blustering wind and the relentless rain soaking the landing, she is not surprised to see the pot of hot pink geraniums knocked to the ground. Searching the entire porch, she can't locate the copper watering can, which she leaves in exactly the same spot each time and she wonders if it too was swept off the windy porch.

Inside now, watering the plants using a drinking glass, she scolds herself for being spooked, realizing it is only because she is alone upstairs and her imagination has grown as wild as the storm outside. Jumping when her phone pings with a text from Andrew, she bursts into a huge smile, viewing one single word, "tomorrow", followed by an exclamation point and a blinking red heart emoji.

Summer storms end as quickly as they erupt in Chicago, and she is not surprised fifteen minutes later to see the wind and rain already dying down as it grows lighter outside. Hurrying down the backstairs, she changes shoes and gathering her purse, races outside to cross the street where she patiently waits at the CTA bus stop, necessitating a final trip to Michigan Avenue to complete her shopping.

Her grandmother's old pearls – check, borrowed beaded purse from the wardrobe mistress at the theater - check, the lacey blue garter – check. All she needs to finish now is to purchase a brand new pair of white satin dress pumps in size nine at Neiman Marcus on Michigan Avenue.

****

After spending her last night as a single woman, she wakes up to perfect weather on her wedding day. Listening to WGN Morning News, she hears Robin, the comical newscaster, talking about Mr. X and laughs along while standing at the stove and scrambling eggs.

Wasting no time, she begins running hot water into the tub and pours in the lavender and eucalyptus crystals, quickly returning to the kitchen to finish washing and drying the breakfast dishes.

Too excited to soak and relax in the dreamy bubble bath, she steps out after a short time and by ten o'clock, finds herself unzipping and carefully slipping into her sophisticated, beaded Carolina Herrera knee-length wedding gown.

The Uber driver springs from the spotless Lincoln Town Car, spouting oohs and ahhs, and he swings open the car door after eyeing the elegant woman cautiously descending the front steps dressed in a stunning wedding gown. It is just past eleven o'clock, and she is seated uncomfortably in the rear seat of the vehicle, attempting not to fidget and wrinkle the gorgeous silk gown as she makes her way to join Andrew at City Hall.

Well, she thinks to herself, that was certainly a bust. Forcing herself to sit perfectly still and barely moving throughout the ride over, Andrew spots her and busting through the crowd, rushes over to pick her up and clasp her in his arms, obviously caring less about wrinkles in a dress. Handsome, he is dressed in his navy Giorgio Armani suit, the one he calls his lucky suit, which always provides a win when wearing it to court.

Her hands shake slightly while she pins the white rose boutonniere onto his lapel as he beams and hands her the delicate wedding bouquet of red roses dotted with baby breath that he chose for her. "Next. Chambers," rings out from the bubbly court clerk holding a clipboard in her hand, and they know it's their turn at bat.

From start to finish, the wedding takes exactly twenty minutes, and Andrew texts the limo driver and photographer to meet them out front, where they will be traveling to the Adler Planetarium, one of the most sought-after venues couples desire for their wedding photographs, showcasing the dramatic backdrop of the Chicago skyline and Lake Michigan.

"When are you going to tell your parents?" she asks. "Probably while sitting at O'Hare sweating it out if our flight departs on time," he laughs. "The only one person I told, and she was sworn to secrecy, was my admin Jeannie, as she had to clear my schedule. It's just our secret, babe."

After making a final stop after the photo session, the limo driver drops them off at her place, where they blissfully climb the stairs together. Andrew stops short to playfully pick her up and carries her over the threshold while she attempts to balance both the pepperoni pizza and bouquet in her hands.

The hot pizza box barely fits on the small wooden table on the back porch, planted between the green mesh patio chairs that they have both plopped down into, and they jubilantly raise their champagne flutes, toasting themselves. Andrew reaches over to wipe the pizza sauce from her mouth, which is about to land on her wedding gown when both are jolted by the sound of his cell phone ringing. No, she shakes her head furiously with her eyes pleading not to answer it, but he does just that, seeing it is a call from Jeannie.

Tenderly holding both of her hands, he lovingly says, "Amy, I promised you nothing would ruin this day and nothing will, but I must leave for the office to witness a Power of Attorney document that is required to be notarized and filed in court today." He assures her he will return as quickly as it takes to drive to his office downtown, sign the necessary paperwork, and immediately return while crossing his fingers that the unpredictable Chicago traffic cooperates. He promises that before she knows it, they will be stepping out of the limo at Terminal One and happily boarding their United flight to Palm Beach, where he vows even though it may only be a short three-day honeymoon, it will be spectacular.

Horns can be heard day and night in the city and they are usually long, angry blasts from furious, irritated motorists. But these are short, quick, happy honks as cars driving by in both directions on Addison Street acknowledge the ecstatic, happy bride and groom locked in a long, passionate kiss in front of her building. Blowing one final kiss at each other, he drives away, and she returns alone to the apartment.

Thinking it best to change into the cropped black jeans and white tie-waist blouse she is planning on traveling in, she carefully steps out of her wedding dress and lays it neatly on her bed while sadly looking at the gorgeous white satin pumps already scuffed and dusty from posing for pictures at the sandy lakefront earlier.

After carrying the leftover pizza and empty champagne glasses into the kitchen, she wipes down the patio table with a Handi Wipe, not wanting to draw any more ants than necessary, and straightens the chairs. It kills her to toss out the uneaten pizza, but with their leaving for Florida, and the Heiser's, who take any leftovers, no matter how old, still on vacation, she stuffs it into a white, plastic garbage bag and pulls the blue drawstrings to secure it tightly.

Returning from the garbage bin in the alley, after dumping the leftovers, she stops to inspect the huge Beefsteak tomatoes

Joseph has planted, which are just now starting to turn red. While looking up to admire the beautiful white and scarlet begonias cascading down from the second-floor planters, she worries the back door appears to be ajar.

After anxiously climbing the stairs to the second floor, she discovers she is mistaken and is relieved to find the door closed and securely locked. Questioning if she should give the begonias another shot of water on this hot day, she changes her mind and goes back downstairs to wait for Andrew.

While rinsing out the crystal flutes and needing to return them to the built-in cut-glass china cabinet in the dining room, she stops, thinking she hears something drop from the apartment upstairs. Refusing to panic, and gazing at the wall clock above the stainless steel refrigerator, she realizes Andrew should be back soon and decides to sit outside on the front steps and wait for him.

However, before she does so, she hears the short, sharp clicks of a woman's high heels descending the back stairs and a sudden, powerful knock on the back door. Too terrified to answer, she is relieved, yet stunned, to hear, "It's just me honey. It's Claudine, now open the door." Turning the key to unlock it, Claudine bursts through the door, pointing a Taser directly at Amy from her outstretched arm. Startled and confused, Amy backs away and is dumbfounded.

"Oh please, don't play little Miss Innocent with me, you ridiculous Steven Spielberg want-to-be. I know it, the world knows it, yet I can't believe Andrew still doesn't know it. You have fought for a decade now and failed miserably to claw your way into our family and prestigious lifestyle. Why do you think he has never married you after all of these years?"

"I nearly died when he humiliated me by getting down on one knee on that filthy hospital floor, and you accepted that ring, until I realized it was the last available tool in his tool box to employ if he wanted to maintain his torrid friends-with-benefits relationship with you."

She madly continues to scream out one grievance after

another, "Do you even realize the scorn and embarrassment I had to endure when my North Shore friends and acquaintances recognized your pathetic photograph in the Lincolnshire Daily Herald wearing those ridiculous, tacky Payless shoes?
 And really, the gall of you, exploring the Chambers Family Monument as if there would ever be a place for you inside it. You were relentless, so I understood months ago, bearing the responsibility of a mother needing to protect her child, that it was my duty to step in."

With each verbal strike slung at her, Amy fearfully takes a step backward, while Claudine aggressively follows with a step forward, and they continue down the hall until they reach Amy's bedroom where an enraged and horrified Claudine gapes at the wedding dress lying on the bed.

Her face flushed with anger, she raises the taser and shoots it at Amy but falls short of hitting her. Her escalating voice booms, "For the love of God, he is five years younger than you! But you just couldn't let him be, could you?"

Sobbing, Amy begs her not to hurt her, explaining it was actually she, Claudine, who inadvertently stemmed Andrew into his desire to marry her after he witnessed the pain and torment she had to endure during the terrifying and life-threatening attacks that she had cruelly orchestrated.

Hearing this only inflames her more so, and exploding with anger, she digs wildly through the bottom of her designer handbag, yanking out a small round pill. With the taser still pointed firmly at Amy, she takes a step back towards the sink, and after dropping the pill into a glass, she fills it with water and angrily demands Amy drink it.

"Be prepared, you little gold digger, to take a final nap in that Jacuzzi you're so proud of. Now move it and march into the bathroom and get undressed!" roars Claudine.

Amy complies, fearful of what a taser can do to her body, and after finishing off the drugged drink, she steps in and sits in the tub. Claudine beams while returning to the living room after turning on the faucets full force, knowing she has successfully achieved her long-sought goal and soon her much-loved son can move on to a woman his equal and worthy of the Chambers name. However, in her madness, she has failed to give thought to where Andrew is, considering they just married, and when she hears the keys jiggling in the front door, her stomach drops.

"Mom," he excitedly shouts, "What are you doing here?" Throwing his arms around her and playfully lifting her into the air, he jokingly kids, "I suppose my beautiful wife has already spilled our big secret. Isn't it fantastic? You've got to be over the moon learning you and Dad are about to become grandparents!"

With a heartbreaking howl and collapsing to the floor, Claudine screams, "Oh my God, what have I done! Andrew call 911!" But already spotting the water spilling out from under the door, he has already charged into the bathroom.

CHRISTINE

It isn't until after 2 AM when the rear lights of the last Lake Zurich police car can be seen departing and driving slowly down the driveway. Christine listens to Charles' weary footsteps as he climbs the winding staircase after locking the door and setting the alarm. Doing her best to forget the nightmare at the pool this evening, she craves sleep but finds herself energized and wide awake.

Lifting the sheet and dragging himself into bed, Charles assures her the officers have made a thorough search of the entire house and grounds and have found nothing suspicious. Still trembling, she asks him to hold her even more tightly than he is and tugging her nightshirt over her head, she rolls over on top of him, seductively rubbing her breasts against his body.

"Not now, Christine," he crossly says. Pushing her aside, he asks again if she is positive she has never seen the woman who attacked her by the pool earlier this evening. Hurt by his rejection, she breaks down and begins to weep, explaining she has never seen this woman before. Furthermore, she is not someone she or anyone else having seen would easily forget. She describes her as a pencil-thin, simple-looking woman appearing to be about thirty years old and wearing a long drab peasant dress, looking like she could be a religious zealot minus the bible.

Christine continues to explain that she was about to switch off the pool lights when her eyes picked up the swishing movement from the drooping branches of the weeping willow tree. Petrified, she observed a strange woman stepping out from under the tree while swatting to keep her tangled hair and mosquitos out of her face. Spotting Christine, her wild feral eyes bore into her with pure hatred. When Christine spun around to run, the strange woman, who was now only inches away, swung the thick limb she was carrying and connected with the back of her head, and at this point, she has no recollection if she fell in the pool or was pushed by the woman.

Hearing one of the kids cry out, she immediately jumps up in bed, but Charles grabs her arm telling her it is Matthew, probably experiencing a nightmare, having been awake throughout most of the evening's terrifying moments. A short time later, she reaches across his body and gently circles her fingers around him, hoping to feel his erection, but her heart sinks when he promptly rolls over, and she hears the bogus snoring as he pretends to have fallen asleep.

****

"Mom, where is my cup," yells Matthew, waking Christine from a deep sleep. Smelling burnt toast and hearing her oldest son trashing through drawers, she struggles to stand up, suffering a horrendous headache. "Just a minute," she yells, "It should be in the plastic basket of sports equipment by the corner window in your room." "Thanks, found it," he yells as she hears him barreling down the stairs.

Popping three Advil, she steps into her flip-flops and follows the trail of burnt toast into the kitchen, where she sees Charles doing his best to feed the rowdy boys breakfast while attempting to get them all out the door by 9 AM for Matthew's little league baseball game.

A flustered Charles greets her and blurts out she should return to bed, as he has everything under control. Glancing around the kitchen, she definitely does not like the looks of everything being under control with milk puddling all over the counter, half-eaten bowls of soggy Lucky Charms, sticky jam stuck on the open jars and burnt toast crumbs covering the floor.

The kids have gone outside and are impatiently waiting to

leave for Matthew's all-important all-star game. Matthew, for the game, and the other kids for the snacks and the awesome playground adjacent to the field.

Frightened to be left alone, she begs Charles to give her fifteen minutes and she will be dressed and ready to join them. However, he insists she stays at home, moaning they are already running late and she shouldn't be out in the sun. "Besides, didn't you just tell me you have a raging headache," he snaps.

She seldom finds her husband in the irritable mood he is in today. Still, she surmises it is only understandable, considering the recent roller coaster of horrors the family has had to ride recently.

Reluctantly she stays home, and after cleaning up the disaster in the kitchen, she retreats upstairs to enjoy a welcomed shower. Positioning herself under the steaming hot water, she adjusts the spray setting on the massager's head and stands under it long enough for it to do its magic and relax and unwind her taut body. Stepping out from the huge walk-in shower, she already feels one hundred percent better and decides it's the perfect day to sit outside on the swing and let her hair dry naturally.

With the Lake Zurich Courier tucked under her arm, she balances a glass of chilled orange juice and a poppy seed bagel slathered in cream cheese and eases down onto the swing. Not long after, knowing she has arrived before she appears, she hears the popping and sputtering from Tammy's noisy muffler, thundering down the driveway.

Tammy flying out of the car, nearly nosedives over Markie's bike, lying in the middle of the yard, and kicks it to the side, yelling, "What the shit. It's no wonder his stupid bike is always getting banged up because this kid is so damn scatterbrained." Crying, she rushes up the steps and into the house, without saying a word. Not due back for another day, Christine presumes she has had an argument with her latest boyfriend.

Her silky hair having dried quickly within fifteen minutes, she gathers up the dishes and heads back to the kitchen to wash them when her cell rings, and she recognizes it's Dana Rae, Charles' pompous executive assistant, calling. Bewildered, as she makes no secret of her disdain for Christine, she knows she would only call in an emergency.

All business as usual, without even a hello, she sputters that she must speak with Charles immediately as she has called three times, and he has failed to pick up, and she goes directly to voicemail. After Christine thoughtfully explains he is at their son's little league game and may have his phone turned off, she hears an obnoxious tsk from the annoying woman and can only imagine her unpleasant rolling eyes.

Dana Rae cautions, "It's probably not my place to disclose this, Christine, but with Charles spending more time than ever at home in Illinois with you and the children, speculation is beginning to snowball that he is seriously dropping the ball. Senator Berger has telephoned twice this past week regarding the foundation's financials. I have had to apologize and stall him with excuses and justifications while waiting for Charles to return. Really, I would think with the boatload of help you have to get through the week you could manage by yourself. I'm sure you are well aware that when even the smallest fire ignites in DC, there are people who thrive on pouring gasoline on top of it, and it can very well be next to impossible to extinguish."

This woman has no clue as to the difficulty of raising four little boys on her own while having a husband who can be gone weeks at a time but bites her tongue and swallows the blood while thanking her and promising to relay the message as soon as he returns home.

When he and the boys do return, after a victory under their belt, with Matthew hitting two doubles, she passes on the message for him to call Dana Rae, commenting on her rudeness and possessiveness. Acknowledging he is well aware of her attitude, he states that she is still the best in the business and is fortunate to have her because many have tried to recruit her.

He admits knowing she called three times during the game, along with a call from the plumber but explains he switched his phone off, just wanting to focus and enjoy watching Matthew's game. It's obvious, and she can see it troubles him to be thought negatively by his peers, and it surprises her to hear the plumber would call him, hoping for not another unexpected surprise.

The boys are jubilant, seeing Tammy's car parked in the driveway and tear up to her corner room, but just as quickly run down, upset by the fact that her door is locked, and they can hear her crying. Charles, lowering his eyes, walks straight past his sons, looking troubled and anxious, not wishing to get involved.

****

Spending more time with Charles is not in the cards after his conversation with Dana Rae yesterday, and she considers herself lucky to receive a cursory peck on the cheek after he helps the limo driver load his bags into the trunk of the sleek vehicle. Sammy has been waiting over an hour to whisk him off to O'Hare Airport to catch the early evening flight back to DC.

"Touched you last, Daddy," giggles Markie as his finger touches Charles' arm while he bends down getting into the car. Pushing his brother out of the way, Matthew yells, "No you didn't, I did," poking his father in the leg. Fighting to squeeze through, Luke wiggles his little arm through his older brothers, touching the hem of Charles' suit pants, and triumphantly screams, "Both of you lose! I touched him last!"

This is the silly game his sons play whenever Charles leaves as they compete to see who can touch him last. She holds on tightly to baby John, who is squirming in her arms and kicking his short, chubby legs, just itching to wiggle loose and join in the game. Wincing, when she finally hears the heavy car door slam shut, praying all little fingers have cleared the door, she hopes there won't be another high-speed chase to the emergency room for stitches.

The boys all lined up like little tin soldiers, jump up and down, waving goodbye to their dad, and she wonders how happy they will be tomorrow when they discover they will be making the agonizing trip to DSW to pick out new school shoes.

Christine finds it hard to believe, but the kids already return to school in two weeks, heralding the end of summer. Weeks ago, having ordered directly through their school, she has already received individual school supply boxes specific to each boy and his grade. Smiling, she recalls how times have changed since the frantic race to get school supplies when she was a girl.

She and her mother would search the aisles at Walgreens, looking for which notebook paper was on sale, being sure not to mistakenly purchase college lined. They would then make the trek all the way out to Zayre's, located at Belmont and Cumberland Avenues at the far end of the city, for special colored pens and pencil cases, and the final trip would be to Sears on Cicero Avenue for her coveted Trapper Keeper, picturing the regal black stallion.

The bribe, lunch at McDonald's for good behavior during shoe shopping, has been unanimously accepted by the fidgety boys, while everyone set to go is growing restless and tired while waiting for Tammy. Crossing their hearts to keep an eye on their antsy baby brother, Christine dashes up the stairs to see what's keeping her this time.

Halfway down the hall, the gagging and retching hits her, and she calls out, asking Tammy if everything is all right. Hearing slow-moving bare feet padding against the hardwood floor, the door cracks open, and holding a white washcloth against her flushed face, Tammy mumbles she feels like crap and not up to making the trip.

"Wait up, boys," she yells as they storm the aisles of DSW while she struggles to untangle baby John's blanket from the wheels of the umbrella stroller. After a frustrating hour of Matthew trying on and being unable to decide between black Nike or black Adidas gym shoes, he finally chooses Nike, and his two younger brothers, of course, want the same exact shoe. With two down, and only having to hunt the correct size for Luke, she unstraps screaming John, who is drawing angry looks from old ladies and teenage clerks alike. He immediately takes off down the aisle, and forgetting the other boys, she chases after him, finding him furiously knocking off shoes from the sales racks. Nerves shot, they troop to the register with cheers of Mickey "D" from the boys while she silently damns Tammy.

****

Broken crayons are tossed across the table and floor throughout the great room, as the children have been painstakingly coloring pictures and get well wishes to slide under Tammy's door for three days now, while Christine grows more frustrated, still having no help from her and only seeing her at mealtimes.

Charles has fallen back to his old ways, and they have been playing phone tag for two days now without a live conversation between them. She is sitting on the front steps, scrolling through Facebook and watching the kids having a rousing game of monkey in the middle, with poor Markie stuck in the middle. Two-year-old John and Tammy are upstairs napping, and lifting her head, she is surprised to see a Lake Zurich patrol car slowly approaching the house.

The boys immediately end the game when a young fresh-faced recruit, sporting a short military haircut, exits the police car, offering up a friendly, "Morning, cowboys." Carrying a large manilla file folder, he strides over to Christine, asking if she has time to view various mug shots of women the department has deemed potential suspects in her attack at the pool.

Shaking her head slowly no, after each photo he passes, she views the four gruesome women, with their smudged eyes and tousled hair, staring out from unflinching eyes, and she regretfully tells him none of these women could possibly have been the same woman who attacked her.

After the police officer leaves, she requests Matthew to run upstairs and check with Tammy if she wants the works on her hot dog, as she plans on zipping over to Max's Dawg House for lunch for herself and the kids. While getting the younger boys firmly belted in place, he returns and jumping into the front seat, announces Tammy is not hungry, and it sounds like she is crying again. Great, Christine thinks, just great, as she shifts the Escalade into drive and takes off down the gravel road.

Bellies full, and everyone smelling of onions, they return home. Pulling into the driveway, she gasps, seeing Tammy's car is missing. Walking back to the house, Luke is the first to spot the tiny, brown toad hopping through the grass. As the other gleeful boys jump in, trying to cup it in their hands, she unlocks the front door and steps inside, hoping to catch sight of a note from Tammy, but she finds none.

The kids pout and grumble when Christine does not allow them to take the captured toad and go down to the pool alone. She promises to take them as soon as John wakes up from his afternoon nap if the weather holds out, but looking up at the ominous clouds rolling across the suddenly darkening sky, it looks doubtful.

When the rain begins to splash down, so also begins the fighting. Giving everyone a half an hour time-out in their respective bedrooms, and while John continues to nap, she throws herself across the soft duvet in her bedroom and enjoying the peace and quiet, drifts off to sleep.

Flying out of bed the moment she hears Markie screaming, she rushes to his bedroom to find the poor child white with fright and is horrified spotting the long ulna bone in his arm broken, as it twists and hangs awkwardly between his elbow and wrist. "Oh my God, what happened, Markie?" she cries as he sobs hysterically, and she is unable to understand a word the child is saying.

Livid with Tammy for acting like some lovesick teenager rather than the thirty-year-old woman she is, she questions the wisdom of allowing her to move in with them in the first place. And as far as Charles, she is twice as angry with him for not paying more attention to her and the family, yet having plenty of time schmoozing with well-heeled donors for his bloody foundation.

Alone and on her own again, she calmly calls for her older sons to put their shoes on and meet her at the front door while she wakes little John from a deep sleep and drags him out of bed.

Getting soaked, the five race to the car as the rain pours

down on them. First, she helps a screaming Markie get seated and situated next to Matthew, who is trying to support his arm. Next, she fights John, who is kicking his legs as she buckles him into his car seat. Finally, she yanks Luke into the front seat, who has been stomping in a huge puddle, wearing his new shoes, and she finds herself on her absolute last nerve.

Struggling to see the road ahead with the windshield blades lashing against the downpour, she calls Charles, which immediately goes to voicemail. Furious, she bangs on the steering wheel and hits the speed dial for Dana Rae, who picks up immediately. She is all too happy to advise Charles is out of the office for the day after requesting she clear his calendar early this morning and only divulges it is for personal reasons.

Inflamed, she blurts out, "I am driving alone in an Illinois monsoon with four little kids, one with a broken arm, and I think it's damn well time Charles place his own flesh and blood over the strangers he so fervently crusades for because if he doesn't get back here soon, he never needs to come back! Got that executive assistant, now get a hold of him and tell him exactly that," and she throws the phone down, swerving just in time to miss the linen truck, exiting the entrance to the emergency room.

They stagger into the emergency room, and the receptionist, taking one look at them, immediately ushers them into a partitioned section where an orderly hurriedly sets up five folding chairs. Squished together in the tiny room, Markie is whisked away by a nurse for X-rays. Thirty minutes later, Dr. Burton pulls the curtain aside, explaining his arm has a compound fracture that will require surgery, and he has admitted the child to the hospital for the night. Christine, insisting on seeing him immediately, is informed by Dr. Burton that the boy has already been sedated and won't be awake until tomorrow morning, so it's probably best she takes the other children home and return then.

Exhausted and arriving back home shortly after eight o'clock, she listens to a cryptic message received on the landline from Tammy, apologizing for what she has done, informing her she had no choice but to follow her heart and hopes she can forgive her. Yet, still no response from Charles.

Matthew is first to run to the window, noticing the dim headlights of the car approaching the house, and excitedly cries out, "Maybe dad is home," and Christine finally grows hopeful. However, when she answers the door, standing there is the same Lake Zurich police officer, sporting the military haircut, she met previously, and he politely asks her to please step outside with him. Confused, she does so, and like lightning, he snaps the heavy handcuffs around her wrists.

The bewildered kids quickly circle their stunned mother as Charles bursts through the patrol car, racing up the stairs to gather the two younger boys in his arms. Matthew, with tears streaming down his face, clings to his mother, sobbing, "Mommy, mama I promise I kept the secret. You know I'm your good boy, and I swear I never told one single person that you have to hurt Markie or Daddy won't love us anymore."

Poised and standing rigid, Christine glares icily at the child and viciously spits in his sweet, innocent face.

BETH

September is completely shocked and visibly shaken, learning Beth cannot possibly be her mother. She goes berserk, realizing her cleverly designed plan has blown up in her face. Not only the money she invested but the intolerable physical pain she inflicted upon herself when faking her rape.

She flashes back, to removing her capris and lying in the dry itchy dead grass, squeezing her eyes tight, as she painfully and furiously drove the jagged Mighty Claw deep into her thighs, ripping the flesh wide open. Nearly passed out from shock, she remembers watching the flies landing one by one and crawling into her open wounds after they caught the scent of the wet blood oozing down her thighs.

Disgusted and left speechless, Beth spots Jessica Torres through the patio doors, and her eyes plead for help. But instead, the bitch is laughing and taunting her by cradling her arms and rocking them back and forth as if holding a baby while pointing her gun at her.

Unexpectantly, catching Beth shift her eyes to the right, September spins around and seeing the shadowy figure of a woman holding a gun presumes the bullet is meant for her. Like a rabid animal, cornered with no way out, she points the gun in the direction of Torres, squeezing the heavy trigger, and with a hail of bullets, blowing out the glass of the patio doors, the woman outside screams out in agony and hits the ground.

Quick to take advantage of the opportunity, Beth charges

September and wrestles her to the ground, grunting as she endlessly smashes her fist into her until the only thing moving on September is the blood pouring from her broken nose. Taking no chances, she runs to the bedroom to retrieve her gun while frantically dialing 911 and yelling into it, "Officer down!"

Catching September's eyes starting to flutter open as she regains consciousness, Beth angrily slams her foot into her chest and holds it there while straining to hear the reassuring sound of sirens, knowing help is on its way.

With sirens wailing, and both red and blue lights flashing, police and emergency responder vehicles speed down the street and arrive simultaneously. Two patrol officers bolt from their squad car, racing into the kitchen and secure the beaten suspect, while Beth rushes into the backyard, joining the harried paramedics sweating over Torres. Observing the two paramedics gazing up at each other, she realizes all hope is gone, and after they place her body into the plastic body bag, the eerie sound of the zipper being drawn up is the only sound to out chirp the crickets on this deadly summer night.

No rush now, the city ambulance slowly drives off with Torres' body, and the swarm of shaken neighbors drift back to the safety of their homes, pondering and discussing how a shooting this horrific could happen in their quiet, peaceful neighborhood.

Alone and standing under the front porch light, Beth spots Torres' black Chevrolet Traverse, which she always kept shining and spotless, even with that long-haired mongrel constantly leaping around inside, parked under the street light a few houses down.

Curiously, she approaches the auto and hears the heart-breaking cries and frenzied whimpering from the dog trapped inside. With only his nose escaping from the slightly cracked window, he seems to sense something horrible has happened and stares out at her with sorrowful, brown eyes. Realizing she dare not open the door to this highly trained canine, she dials headquarters, explaining the tragic situation. She advises she needs immediate assistance, especially not knowing how long the animal has been locked in the hot, sweltering vehicle.

****

The following morning, glancing up and down the street, she notices she is the last of her neighbors to retrieve the Chicago Sun-Times lying in the driveway. Barefoot, she pads across the hot cement to pick it up, and opening it before even returning inside, she gasps at the sky-high headline jumping out at her – One watch commander, three captains and four lieutenants from Districts 1, 18 and 25 have been indicted for bribes and money laundering, with more names to follow.

Back at work, she slips a twenty dollar bill into the manilla envelope and signs her name, donating to Torres' favorite charity, St. Jude, per her mom and dad's wishes, just as Captain Washington approaches her asking, "Got a minute to grab a coffee Ooh La La?" Saying not a word, she rises from her desk and follows him to the vending machines. Carrying the steaming coffee, she follows him into his office where after shutting the door and closing the dusty window blinds, he politely asks her to take a seat.

Nervous and on edge, her right foot jiggles up and down as he sits solemnly in front of her, not uttering a word. Without warning, he reaches out and stretches his arm across the desk to vigorously shake her hand, blurting out, "Good job, Crowley. I was advised by the fifth floor, only this morning, that the Feds recruited you, and you were working undercover on this momentous corruption investigation. I applaud you, kid. You had me worried, knowing I talked you into taking the exam and then you scoring so high and landing near the top of the list." Throwing her head back, relieved and laughing, she quips, "Shit, you were worried, I was worried that maybe that big old mitt of yours was in the piggy bank and you might be involved in the payoffs."

She details the captain on how the Federal Bureau of Investigation secretly contacted her after they determined from inside sources that she had no desire to move up CPD ranks, as she was perfectly content being a detective getting her hands dirty fighting street crime. With her ruthless reputation, they felt confident that at her age, suddenly developing a taste for promotion, the sharks would be circling the water, charging her an exorbitant amount of money to land high on the list.

"I agreed because I got so damn sick of watching all those highly qualified, honest cops getting the shaft, never having a fair shot at promotion, while those lazy, arrogant, clout-heavy pricks waltz right in not knowing shit about the job. And I only pray they bust that slime-ball Tony's macho balls, the jag-off demanding not only an exorbitant amount of money from me but also kinky sex for the promotion," she snaps.

"Ain't gonna happen, kid," says the captain, "He's already sung like the little girl canary he is taking down Tommy Burke, the Watch Commander." "Cap," she groans, "Can you please explain to me why the hell a decorated watch commander even gets his hands dirty with the chance of losing his pension for a few measly bucks? Is it true money is the root of all evil?" "No, but the love of money sure as hell is," answers the world-weary captain.

"I know some guys are gonna despise me when this all hits the fan, and I'll be pegged with a new nickname "La Rat", but they're the same arrogant, conniving pricks who I never thought much of in the first place, and I'll take comfort knowing I have earned the respect of many of my honorable, hard-working fellow officers, and quite frankly, Scarlet I really, really don't give a damn."

"I think the world of you, Ooh La La, and I've already approved your transfer request, but if there is anything else I can ever do for you, you only need to ask," he affectionately says. And with this being said, she lights up, hoping to hear just those very words.

EPILOGUE

(Eight weeks later)

Amy

Torn and shredded sparkly gift wrap, along with blue and white ribbons and perfect bows, are strewn across the floor in front of them as Amy and Andrew rise, holding hands and thank everyone for their adorable and generous baby gifts while attending the amazing shower in their honor today.

Too excited to wait, they know that come next spring, a little Andy Jr. will be cushioned in his stroller, gurgling and drooling down his blue "I Love the Cubbies" sweatshirt when the proud trio marches down Greenwood Avenue under the canopy of sugar maple trees.

Surprising Donna, Amy summons her tireless production assistant to join them, announcing, "We especially want to thank Donna for her tireless effort to make this day perfect in every way, and to also congratulate and wish her well after receiving a well-earned promotion to Head of Guest Services at the Meridian's Orlando World Center." Then hugging her tightly, she plops a pair of sparkling red sequined Mickey Mouse ears on top of her head.

Shortly afterward, an out-of-breath Poppy flies into the banquet room just as the other guests are packing up their unique honey jar favors with "Baby to Bee" scrawled across them and saying their goodbyes. Forever bundled in drama, she rushes over to Amy and profusely apologizes for being late while beaming and gushing that she has landed the role of Jasmine in the Cadillac Palace Theater production of *Aladdin* and lost time studying her lines. Handing her an organic cotton sleeper, with the tags still attached, and stuffed into the bottom of a red and white Macy's bag, she begs forgiveness for not having time to wrap it.

Balancing the cuddly, white teddy bear on top of the last of the boxed gifts, Andrew loads them into the Lexus and grows emotional, thinking of how his mother would have loved this day. She is no doubt humiliated, knowing her friends and family are enjoying each other's company and celebrating the coming birth of her first grandchild, while she sits home alone as an outcast, reflecting on her disgraceful actions, with the realization that even after years of therapy, she may never see the child.

Claudine managed to avoid criminal actions, given the fact Amy did not want to estrange the family by pressing charges. However, she still refuses to see or speak to her mother-in-law, especially after she broke down admitting she had hired a thug to stalk Amy, who not only attacked and terrified her while disguised as a monk, but also engineered the chilling episode of setting ablaze all the lights in her two-flat.

She also confessed to orchestrating other appalling acts, such as hiring the elderly Uber driver to honk his horn endlessly outside her home at 2 AM, and the sly bell boy at the Meridian to steal her shoes and break into her file cabinet, amongst other troubling deeds.

However, nothing compares to her personally clubbing Amy over the head outside the Chambers Family Mausoleum or forcibly drugging her while attempting to murder her and her unborn grandson.

Andrew's father sadly recounts to Amy and Andrew the time he first met Claudine years ago. Never coming from money, she was just out of high school working as a salesgirl in the Mister Shop at the Harlem-Irving Plaza. While he was closely scrutinizing a bold tie, Claudine playfully whipped it from his hands and replaced it with the most expensive tie in the store and easily persuaded him to purchase it.

Being beautiful, it was easy to fall in love with the attractive, fun-loving girl, but he quickly discovered after marrying her that she was a social climber who believed money gave her the license to be rude and arrogant. Bitterly, he explains she knew the price of everything, but the value of nothing and believed her snobbery was a sign of strength.

Amy doesn't say a word, never wishing to see this despicable woman again, while Andrew lovingly thanks his dad for the endearing gift of a junior fishing pole for his grandson, with the promise of them spending happier summers fishing off the shores of Lake Michigan at their country home in charming Door County.

Christine

Gorgeous yellow leaves flutter to the sidewalk from the stately Chinese Elm tree in front of their new home in the historic Georgetown neighborhood, where the kids have adapted amazingly, making new friends at the Sidwell Friends School.

"Dad, Dad come quick and look at this," cries Markie, dragging him to the huge display of Halloween costumes. Charles finds himself enjoying shopping with the excited boys for creepy costumes and scary decorations for the upcoming Halloween holiday.

Leaving the unspeakable nightmare behind, Christine is now locked securely away in a woman's mental health facility in Chicago, not far from her mother, not knowing if she will ever reunite with her family.

Never revealing by what means he discovered she was abusing the boys, he remembers the day well when Cookie, the plumber, contacted him while watching Matthew's Little League game and shared with him her suspicions about the abuse. She believed a kid would flush toys down the toilet for attention but never his favorite, and it was obvious to her, the times she observed the boy interacting with his mother, that he was clearly afraid of her when she hugged him way too tightly, trying to console him by smothering him with affection. On the day Christine complained about the vicious note she received from Markie, she pointed out it was placed on the top shelf of the medicine cabinet, which Cookie knew the child could never have reached.

Learning this, he immediately contacted Tammy, who finally with great difficulty, admitted she had the same thoughts but felt she had an obligation to stay loyal to her friend. The fact that these suspicions were beginning to make her physically ill was the final realization that she had a responsibility to notify or share this information with the authorities.

He then arrived at the grim conclusion that no one except Christine and the children were present when these horrific acts occurred. Looking back, he realized how simple it was for her to fake a head injury and throw herself into the family swimming pool, but how insane was it to painfully slice into her own skin after the gala, which she eventually admitted to doing.

And then there was poor Markie. What kind of mother inflicts pain on her own flesh and blood, especially a poor innocent child, going as far as drugging him and cruelly raising a heavy mallet and slamming it down on his arm? He bore the brunt of his mother's horrific physical abuse. Still, Matthew is just as broken, suffering from the emotional anguish caused by feeling the need to keep her secret to save the family from losing their father's love. Both boys have years of therapy ahead of them but are slowly healing while being treated by the compassionate child psychiatrists of MedStar Georgetown University Hospital.

Charles is now aware Christine suffers from Munchausen Syndrome by Proxy. MSP can affect anyone but is most commonly seen in mothers of children six years old and under. Since Christine appeared to be caring and attentive, doctors never suspected her of any wrongdoing. However, having an overwhelming need for attention, she went to great lengths to achieve it, even if it meant risking her son's life. It is also believed that individuals with MSP enjoy the satisfaction of deceiving people they perceive to be more powerful than themselves, and in her case, it was Charles.

The doctors expressed she most likely experienced a traumatic incident when she was a child, which never having been addressed nor receiving any support caused her great fears of abandonment, which carried over into adulthood. Charles, however, is adamant this is not the case, knowing she would have shared any such life-altering details with him. He contends she had a perfectly normal childhood and was raised in a stable home environment by two loving parents.

Tammy has been graciously living in and maintaining the Lake Zurich house, and with a healthy bid on the table, it should be sold any day now. She has also made the arduous drive into Chicago to visit Christine, only to find her duplicating her mother by sitting frozen in her chair, blankly staring out the window while clutching an open bible in her nail-bitten hands.

Markie is still Markie, and he is now questioning Charles if he thinks Dana Rae might be thinking of doing him in just to collect his treasured autographed Cubs baseball.

Beth

September's jury trial for the murder of Officer Jessica Torres is scheduled to begin next week. This being the first time Beth will come face to face with her since the senseless killing of Torres, she is hopeful it will be the last, knowing September is staring down life in prison at best.

Pleased that her transfer came through to District 22, she now actively investigates crime in her own neighborhood but still misses the old crew at 25, especially Captain Washington.

When boxing up her belongings from the beat-up desk in her old office and lugging them across town to her new, even more dilapidated desk, there was one thing she had hoped to leave behind. Nevertheless, on the first day reporting to work, she was welcomed with a huge blue and white eight-foot banner greeting her with "Welcome to Paris Ooh La La!"

She knows the Floridians would be pleased, especially Mama Bear, seeing the red GMC Sierra backing into her driveway. It feels good to be back together, and jumping up to open the door before he even hits the first step, she calls out and teases, "Danny, my man, so glad to see you made it on time." Right back at her, he banters, "Yeah, if I hadn't, I know you'd be all too happy to kick my sweet ass. Ready to go #79?"

"Hey, are we ready to go?" she yells. Magnum tears down the hall, clenching his leash in his mouth. Barreling through the front door, he leaps into the back of the GMC, whining excitedly, knowing exactly where they're going - to enjoy the day and join his other four-legged buddies splashing and bucking the cold Lake Michigan waves at sunny Montrose Avenue Dog Beach.

Sister Eleanor

Marlena cautiously rolls Sister Eleanor's wheelchair onto the rickety wooden porch of St. Philomena's to enjoy the brisk fall air and witness the brilliantly colored red and orange maple leaves. Sister is slowly recovering from the grave stroke that paralyzed the right side of her body. It is a daily challenge just to chew her food, and she struggles when trying to communicate, having only the use of the left side of her mouth.

Like countless stroke victims, she travels in and out of reality. On any given day, she may believe she is a different age and is transformed back to that particular place and year of her life.

Two weeks ago, Marlena found her sobbing. When questioning her why, Sister Eleanor, believing she was eight years old, cried it was because she didn't write her letters correctly, and old Sister Magda, her third-grade teacher at St. Hedwig's in 1947, had hoisted her ruler and came down hard, striking her fingers.

The week before, she was solidly ensconced in the year 1959

and was a giddy nineteen-year-old, explaining to Marlena how exciting it was to be a young postulant after seeking admission to the Sisters of St. Casmir Order in Chicago at the same time the country was celebrating both Alaska and Hawaii becoming the United States 49th and 50th states.

During the doctor's last visit, he asked her three questions. Her name, which she answered correctly; her address, which she answered correctly; and the third question, what year it was and who is the current president of the United States, to which she proudly proclaimed, "Silly, it's 1963 and every good Catholic knows John Fitzgerald Kennedy, our first Roman Catholic president, currently occupies the White House."

However, in recent days, she has experienced a deterioration of her health, and it is even more difficult for her to communicate. Still capable of reading, she enjoys and spends most days browsing through Catholic periodicals and the Chicago newspapers.

After massaging her arthritic hands and making sure they are warm, Marlena places the Chicago Sun-Times in her lap. Under the front page headline, a mug shot stares out of the horrible woman who was arrested for killing the female Chicago police officer a few months back.

After returning with Sister's hot tea and lemon, she finds her animated and frustrated, mumbling a jumble of grunts and groans but unable to get her words out of her mouth while her left finger stabs at the woman in the photograph. Marlena, knowing Sister could not possibly know this woman, tucks the blanket around her legs to keep her warm and then shuts the screen door as she goes back inside.

Sister Eleanor, now believing it is September 1992, instantly notices the girl in the newspaper. It would be impossible not to recognize her. However, the photo doesn't do her justice, and she looks more like a thirty-year-old woman than the sixteen-year-old girl she is. It's the same pregnant girl who gave birth this morning to a six-pound, four-ounce baby girl that was adopted by the loving elderly couple from Iowa; the first

Alphabet Girl who arrived weeks ago with her crushed sugar cube corsage, sweet little Amy.

The End

ACKNOWLEDGEMENT

Without Grandma Kuchl, this book would never have been possible. Lucky enough to spend my childhood summers at her Lake George country house in Wisconsin, along with an entire gang of crazy cousins, it was her steadfast rule of forbidding a television that caused endless moaning from us kids. Whenever we would grumble and complain, she would shoo us out the screen door on hot summer evenings to sit under the stars, urging us to use our imaginations and tell stories. And unfortunately for my cousins, mine were always scary.

Ryan, my wonderful grandson and the joy of my life, whom I love to the moon and back, this book would never have been written without your leaving for freshman year at Illinois State University. Because I worried about your mother becoming an empty nester, my only goal in writing this book was to keep her distracted from missing you by keeping her busy editing it.

Well, my dear daughter, you found out it wasn't so bad being an empty nester, and I discovered a passion for writing. Without a doubt, I have been blessed with the most wonderful daughter in the world. You are my hero! You are the woman I always strived to be, but it is you who has succeeded.

Many thanks to you dear Bob, and my comedian son Jim, who is hysterically funny and never fails to keep the family in stitches.

It is wonderful knowing both of you always have my back without words ever needing to be spoken.

Everyone has a best friend, and mine is the very best. Thank you, Marlene, my lifelong buddy since kindergarten, who has traveled with me down this road called life. Never having a bad word to say about anyone or anything, I appreciate the tough time you must have had to critique me, but you did just that, and I thank you for it.

Thank you to my dear Italiano friend Viv, who is just as tough as this German fräulein. If anyone would give me honest opinions, I knew it was you, and I will always be grateful for your encouragement, knowing damn well I had better follow through and not disappoint you.

And very special thanks to Kerry, Marlene's incredible daughter, who is every bit as sweet as she is talented, for creating and designing this amazing book cover.

Last but not least, thanks to Danny, my favorite real-life Chicago police officer, who took time out from his busy life and golf game to provide me advice regarding the bad guys.

BOOKS BY THIS AUTHOR

Coming Soon........
Whistling At The Top Of The Stairs

Returning after fifty years to her childhood home on the North Side of Chicago and immersed in fond memories and waves of nostalgia, the feisty senior is horror-stricken while witnessing a shocking murder on her first day back in the city. She is thrust into the center of a mysterious death that is sparked by her return and cryptically revolves around her. After moving back into the familiar century-old two-flat in the charming Roscoe Village neighborhood, she discovers it is just the beginning of terrifying acts and deceptions soon to target her. Horrified to hear the chilling whistling for the first time, it quickly rekindles her fears of a lifetime ago, especially those of the ominous basement that so terrorized her as a child. Having been away for decades it is unfathomable to imagine anyone harboring such hatred for her, and she painstakingly struggles to discover who wants her dead.

Made in the USA
Las Vegas, NV
04 February 2025

17480875R00095